CAST OF C

Bill Runson. A decent, hard-worl
his relatives.

Eliot Runson. His hard-drinking, carefree cousin, who is also Bill's employee.

Irene Wisner. Bill's fun-loving, glamorous former stepmother.

Madeleine Smith. Irene's daughter, who used to bully Bill when they were younger.

Mrs. Goodhue. Bill's bossy but capable housekeeper.

Mrs. Reilly. Her erstwhile replacement, who claims that Bill looks exactly like her deceased son.

Joe Reilly. Her surviving son, a delicate young man given to fainting spells.

Dykes. The police detective in charge of the investigation.

Gus and Hank. His assistants.

Inavsy. A concert whistler, whom we never meet.

Books by Constance & Gwenyth Little

The Grey Mist Murders (1938)
Black-Headed Pins (1938)
The Black Gloves (1939)
Black Corridors (1940)
The Black Paw (1941)
The Black Shrouds (1941)
The Black Thumb (1942)
The Black Rustle (1943)
The Black Honeymoon (1944)
Great Black Kanba (1944)
The Black Eye (1945)
The Black Stocking (1946)
The Black Goatee (1947)
The Black Coat (1948)
The Black Piano (1948)
The Black Smith (1950)
The Black House (1950)
The Blackout (1951)
The Black Dream (1952)
The Black Iris (1953)
The Black Curl (1953)

All titles reprinted by The Rue Morgue Press

The Black Curl

By Constance & Gwenyth Little

Rue Morgue Press
Lyons / Boulder

About the Littles

And then were none.

The publication of *The Black Curl* marks the end of our program to bring the mysteries of these two Australian-born sisters back into print. Although all but one of their books had "black" in the title, the 21 mysteries of Constance (1899-1980) and Gwenyth (1903-1985) Little were far from somber affairs. The two sisters from East Orange, New Jersey, were far more interested in coaxing chuckles than in inducing chills from their readers.

Indeed, after their first book, *The Grey Mist Murders*, appeared in 1938, Constance rebuked an interviewer for suggesting that their murders weren't realistic by saying, "Our murderers strangle. We have no sliced-up corpses in our books." However, as the books mounted, the Littles did go in for all sorts of gruesome murder methods—"horrible," was the way their own mother described them—which included the occasional sliced-up corpse.

But the murders were always off stage and tempered by comic scenes in which bodies and other objects, including swimming pools, were constantly disappearing and reappearing. The action took place in large old mansions, boarding houses, hospitals, hotels, or on trains or ocean liners, anywhere the Littles could gather together a large cast of eccentric characters, many of whom seemed to have escaped from a Kaufman play or a Capra movie. The typical Little heroine—each book was a stand-alone—often fell under suspicion herself and turned detective to keep the police from slapping the cuffs on. Whether she was a working woman or a spoiled little rich brat, she always spoke her mind, kept her rather sarcastic sense of humor, and got her man, both murderer and husband. But if marriage was in the offing, it was always on her terms and the vows were taken with more than a touch of cynicism. Love was grand, but it was even grander if the husband could either pitch in with the cooking and cleaning or was wealthy enough to hire household help.

The Littles wrote all their books in bed—"Chairs give one backaches," Gwenyth complained—with Constance providing detailed plot outlines while Gwenyth did the final drafts. Over the years that pattern changed somewhat, but Constance always insisted that Gwen "not mess up my clues." Those clues were everywhere, and the Littles made sure there were no loose ends. Seemingly irrelevant events were revealed to be of major significance in the final summation. The plots were often preposterous, a fact often recognized by both the Littles and their characters, all of whom seem to be winking at the reader, almost as if sharing a private joke. You just have to accept the fact that there are different natural laws in the wacky universe created by these sisters. There are no other mystery writers quite like them. At times, their books seem to be an odd collaboration between P.G. Wodehouse and Cornell Woolrich.

The Littles published their two final novels, *The Black Curl* and *The Black Iris*, in 1953, and the books they published in the 1950s were pale imitations of their first books from the 1930s and 1940s. They were shorter, less complicated and simply not as funny as classics such as *The Black Shrouds* or *Great Black Kanba*. In their final books they played around with shifting point of view and often employed a male as the central character, perhaps to meet the demands for more male-oriented mysteries required by the post World War II reading public. They certainly were listening to their editors at the Doubleday Crime Club when it came to plotting. The Russian roulette scene in *The Black Iris* was put there because a Crime Club artist had a scene he wanted to use for the cover. If they missed writing, they were at least able to devote more time to their real passion—traveling. The two made at least three trips around the world at a time when that would have been a major undertaking. For more information on the Littles and their books, see the introductions by Tom & Enid Schantz to The Rue Morgue Press editions of *The Black Gloves* and *The Black Honeymoon*.

Chapter One

BILL RUNSON WAS FROWNING AT A TELEGRAM WHEN HIS cousin Eliot Runson walked into his office. Eliot was breezy, and ignoring both the frown and the telegram, said, "Cheer up, Bill. You haven't lost everything. I'm here."

"What do you want, now? I'm busy."

Eliot seated himself on a corner of the desk and swung his leg. "It isn't business because I haven't been to my desk yet. I deferred the pleasure so that I might come in here and cheer you up. You always need cheering on a Friday—Sunday holiday looming up. Poor Bill."

"Shut up and get out of here," Bill said briefly.

"What's in the telegram? Someone canceled an order? You'll need sleeping pills for a week."

"If you don't intend to do any work today, as usual," Bill said grimly, "go and entertain someone else."

Eliot lit a cigarette and grinned through the smoke. "Actually, all I need is a measly hundred dollars."

Bill crashed his fist down onto the desk. "For God's sake! Why do you cut it so fine? You get a good salary, and yet you're obliged to borrow constantly. You know what your income is. Why don't you live within it?"

"Well, I love a good time the way you love work. I'll admit

that I shouldn't have bought the new car. I'd have been all right without that, but I'm not in such bad shape. All I need is the hundred, and then I can straighten myself out and pay it back in a couple of months."

"Why does everyone pick on me?" Bill demanded bitterly, apparently addressing the top of his desk. "People who should have plenty. I deny myself things so that I can pay my bills, and then I have to shell it out anyway to people who can't say no when they want something."

Eliot raised his eyebrows. "Er, has someone else been trying to put the bite on you, too?"

"Yes."

Eliot sighed. "I won't deny that it's a blow to me. I've always considered you my own private source. If you'll put a name to this character, I'll go and set him back on his heels."

"No, you won't." Bill unfolded the telegram and handed it over.

"AM TERRIBLY BROKE. MAY WE STAY AT YOUR HOUSE FOR A BARE WEEK. ARRIVE NINETEENTH. IRENE."

Eliot slid into a chair, grinning wickedly. "You quiet ones! I had no idea you knew any girl well enough to assume that she could stay at your home, even for a bare week. She says 'we,' of course. Perhaps she has a husband with her?"

"No. She's out of husbands for the moment. Be getting a fresh one in shortly. She refers to her big, bullying daughter. I'm two years older than this monstrosity, but she was bigger and taller when we were kids, and she knocked me about at will. My loathing for her would interest a psychiatrist."

"It interests me." Eliot was still amused. "So Irene's just an elderly dame, after all. Do I know her?"

"Of course you know her. She was married to my father for a few years. Dad wanted a mother for his boy, so he used his well-known intelligence and picked Irene. I saw her only once or twice when she was supposed to be mothering me, but since I've grown up, she insists on lunching with me every time she passes through town."

Eliot gave a long, low whistle. "*That* babe. I remember her coming in here, but I didn't know she was your ex-mother. She's no elderly dame—what are you frowning for? Send her over to me. I'll give her houseroom for a week."

"Nothing doing," Bill said grimly. "I'd agree gladly, except that I'd have to give you a measly thousand instead of a hundred, and I can't afford it. As far as I'm concerned, she can sit at home for the week, or pay for her own amusement. I'm not taking her out anywhere. She has a damned nerve, anyway. If today weren't the nineteenth, I'd get in touch with her and put her off. She was too smart for that, though. She probably sent the telegram just before she got into the taxi to go to my house. I haven't heard from Mrs. Goodhue yet, but she'll be calling me at any minute."

Eliot nodded. "You'll hear from the old lemon. In fact, she'll probably hand in her notice. People messing up the house and sitting on her plumped up cushions. She has me trained to a hard chair. She spies on me through a crack in the door, and if I leave the chair for anything softer, she comes scuttling in and hovers until she can get at the dent I've made. I'm afraid to ask her for so much as a glass of water. Matter of fact, I'd rather do all the work myself. I don't know how you stand it."

Bill scowled and reached for his clamoring telephone. He said, "Yes?" and then, "Oh, yes, Mrs. Goodhue. Yes. I received the telegram only a short while ago myself." He frowned at Eliot, who was laughing quietly. "Just make up two bedrooms, please, before you leave, and put the guests in them, and when I get back I'll give you your money and a reference."

He banged down the receiver, and thundered at Eliot, "Haven't you anything to do this morning?"

"Yes, boss." Eliot hauled his tall slim length from the chair. "Only you shouldn't make things so entertaining in your office if you want me to go to mine."

"Well, get out."

"I'm glad she's leaving," Eliot said, moving towards the door. "Now I can visit you in peace. Would you like me to dig up another scullery maid for you?"

"No."

"O.K. I'll leave you to your morning of faithful, steady work. You're your father's own son, and can you feature the old man getting his feet tangled up with *Irene* as a mother for his boy!"

The telephone rang again, and Bill was silent for some time after he had answered it, while a feminine voice crackled against his ear. Eliot paused at the door, straining his ears, and presently Bill said, "From five to six is the soonest I can get home. I'll see you then, Irene," and put down the receiver.

Eliot slid out of the door, and Bill looked down at his desk with his head clutched in his hands. He'd really have to sell the house. He owned a good business and had a brownstone house in a good part of town, so everyone thought he was wealthy. Hadn't they ever heard of taxes, or didn't they pay theirs? He liked the house. He'd been born and brought up in it and he hated the thought of going into an apartment. Be a lot cheaper, though. Only, he *could* afford the house, even with all the obligations it entailed, if it were not for people like Eliot and Irene. There were an endless stream of them, with endless invitations, and they all had one idea: to get some money out of him.

He straightened up and slapped the flat of his hand onto the desk. He'd keep the house, and fight them all—fight for his rights—and Irene would be the first on the list. She could stay the one bare week she had mentioned, and only that, and if she wanted to run any parties, she'd get a flat No. Let her mess up someone else's house with cigarette burns and alcohol stains. He shook his head a little and got down to the work of the day.

He started for home at half past five and went to the subway as usual. It wasn't as pleasant as a cab, but it was faster and cheaper. Sometimes he was even able to get a seat. The car thinned out as he approached his station, and he glanced casually at the middle-aged woman who sat directly opposite. She was on the elderly side, comfortably plump, simply dressed, and with neat, gray hair. She was looking down, and Bill's glance lingered to dislike the hat she was wearing. All right, perhaps, except for the bunch of cherries on the side.

She looked up suddenly and met his eyes, and he saw her mouth drop open while a confusion of astonishment and almost fear spread over her face.

Chapter Two

BILL LOOKED AWAY QUICKLY, AND THEN REALIZED THAT THE train was pulling into his station. He stood up, and as he made for the door, he was conscious of the woman making her way along behind him.

He bought a paper on the street and stood for a few moments, looking over the headlines, before turning in the direction of his home. He walked slowly, reflecting, rather gloomily, that he'd have to listen to Mrs. Goodhue, Irene, and perhaps that bullying daughter as well.

Someone was walking behind him, footsteps with a limp, and he glanced back. He saw the cherries on her hat first, and then recognized her as the elderly woman who had been on the subway. Must live in the neighborhood; perhaps she'd realized that she knew him when she saw him in the subway. He should have nodded to her. Well, it was unimportant, anyway. He mounted the steps, and went in to his house.

There were immediate sounds of talk and laughter, and he set his jaw. Naturally. Irene couldn't sit and read a book. There wouldn't be time. She picked up the latest on books in general conversation and then pretended that she'd read them. No use standing around stewing over an old resentment that went back to the time she'd been his mother and the bully had been his sister. Irene had her good points, if you wanted to be strictly fair. She was cheerful and gay, and he had never had a cross word from her.

He wondered what color her hair was this time, and it was the first thing he looked for when he entered the parlor.

It wasn't bad, a light brown with golden glints, much better than the platinum blonde her hair had been the last time he'd taken her to lunch—better than the yellow blonde, the golden and red, and the jet black. In fact, this was really rather nice.

Irene yelled, "Darling! How nice you look! Actually, you are my favorite son."

"Hello, Irene. I didn't know you had any other sons."

She was surrounded by three men, two who were strangers to Bill and Eliot. Bill looked at him sourly and asked, "How did *you* get here so soon?"

"The business isn't mine," Eliot said reasonably, "so I usually sneak out a few minutes before the bell rings."

Irene introduced Bill and the two men, but gave them no time to acknowledge the introduction. She handed Bill a martini, and one of the strangers murmured, "Really, Irene, the way you mix a martini makes me shudder."

"Oh, *Bill* won't know the difference. He'll probably forget to drink it, anyway."

Eliot shook his head. "He couldn't stand the waste."

Bill glanced down at the glass in his hand. "Well, if I don't drink it now, I'll put it in the refrigerator and finish it tomorrow."

One of the guests unexpectedly found this hilariously funny, while the other was inclined to be a bit sober over an irreverence to what he considered a high art. He collected the laugher, and they departed after making a couple of dates to take Irene to dinner, at her insistence. She declared that they should make two dates because they were two people, and added that they couldn't camp here forever, because the place belonged to her adored son, Bill.

"I don't know why you make a point of telling people that I'm your son," Bill said mildly. "You're beginning to look younger than I do."

"Yes, I know, darling, but people dig up things. If I admit freely that you are my son—well, my stepson—they merely think that I married an old man for his money."

Bill took a sip of his drink, and Eliot murmured, "I'm still here. Do I have to go, too?"

Irene blew him a kiss. "My dear, you're wonderful! I simply adore you! How old are you?"

"Oh, well"—Eliot waved a hand—"what's age between two souls?"

Irene laughed and put her arm through his, and Bill asked her, "Will you be in for dinner tonight?"

She extended the toe of one shoe and made a little face at it. "Just this one evening? All right?"

Bill nodded. "I'll tell Mrs. Goodhue."

He went into the hall and towards the back sitting room, and Irene clapped a hand over her mouth and rolled her eyes at Eliot.

Mrs. Goodhue was not in the back sitting room, a place where she was usually to be found in between violent flurries of household activity, but the bully was there. Bill knew her at once.

She was different, though. Bill stopped and stared while she gave him an impatient frown. She had acquired beauty. Dark hair framed a smooth, lovely face, and she wore a dull blue suit that depended on its own smart lines for distinction. There were no obvious buttons, and it did not sparkle anywhere. She wore no makeup, save a little lipstick.

She observed, without much interest, "You've changed a lot."

Bill found himself suffused by a feeling of well-being. He smiled and walked over to her. "Not as much as you. See? I'm taller than you are now."

She raised one shoulder in an indifferent gesture. "Too bad. I used to have the upper hand."

"But, Madeleine—" He was trying to articulate a profound surprise. "You—well, you don't look anything like Irene."

"How do you know? Mother changes her appearance so frequently that nobody can be sure what she looks like."

He gave it up and asked almost aggrievedly, "Why didn't you come to any of those lunches your mother's been sticking me for?"

Her gray eyes darkened, and she turned a little away from him. "In the first place, Mother doesn't like me to tag along on her dates, but more important, *I* don't like sticking anybody for anything. I'm thoroughly annoyed at being here because I know that you didn't invite us, as Mother said. She declared that you *in-sisted*."

"Well, I—"

Madeleine nodded. "Yes, that's what I thought. I know what she's up to, and she's not going to get away with it."

"Don't get annoyed with her," Bill said easily. "She's good company, you know, and she has her own way of doing things. I'm glad that you're staying here with me."

"You won't be when you find out what she's trying to wangle."

"She said she was broke and needed a place to stay for a week."

"Why—" Madeleine's voice rose a little. "That was a deliberate lie. She's made money from several marriages, and she takes the utmost care of it. You may be surprised to learn that she has a nice fat, steady income."

Bill whistled softly. "I'm glad to hear it, of course, but in that case, why *did* she come here? Is she stingy with her money?"

"No. She's quite generous, really, and as far as her dates are concerned, she sticks only those who can afford it. It isn't that. It's just that she's been looking around for a desirable husband for me, and I believe she thinks you'd do."

She expected him to laugh or become embarrassed, but he merely looked puzzled. "You mean she'd go to all that trouble? But she knows masses of men all over the world."

"Oh, yes, but she's very selective. She's served me several dishes already that I've eeled around. If I haven't forgotten one, you're number five. You did *not* insist that we come here to stay?"

"No," Bill admitted. "I heard nothing of it until this morning, and I'll be honest enough to tell you that I was annoyed. But I'm still being honest when I add that I'm no longer annoyed, that, in fact, I'm very pleased. I like being dish number five."

"It's disgusting," Madeleine said flatly, "but I can't do anything with her. Only I do promise to get her out of here within the week."

Irene and Eliot appeared at the doorway, and Irene gave Bill and her daughter a careful glance before she said gaily, "Bill, this Eliot is a perfect *love*. You should have unveiled him before."

"I've been saving him for New Year's Eve."

"Mother," Madeleine said coldly, "you know Mrs. Goodhue has left, and I think we should go so that Bill can get her back. It's very hard to get help these days."

"My dear, I *know*, and that's why I *always* live in a hotel. I realize that it's pleasant to have your own place, with your own things about—but the work! We shall just have to go out for dinner."

"No, we won't," Madeleine said grimly. "If you insist on foisting us on Bill, then you and I will do the work ourselves."

Irene squeezed Eliot's arm and giggled. "She's quite mad. She can't cook one single thing, and nor can I."

"We'll go out," Bill said hastily. "Eliot can come, and we'll make a night of it." He turned to Madeleine and added, "I'd really enjoy it. I don't go out very often. You run upstairs now, and we'll leave as soon as you're ready."

"Dears!" Irene smiled around at all of them. "How delightful."

Madeleine shrugged. "All right, Bill, you stuck your neck out, but remember, when we come down ready, you won't be able to take us to the corner drugstore."

She went off with Irene, and Eliot laughed. "You'll have to pull out the evening raiment, boy. Shake it free of moth balls. If you'll excuse me, I'll dash home and drape my form suitably, and bow out of my own private date. When the boss asks you out for the evening as an escort for an extra girl, you can't very well refuse."

Bill said, "Besides, it's cheaper because the boss is expected to pay, under those circumstances. Only don't think you're going to make much time with Irene. You're just a salaried man."

Eliot had got as far as the door, but he stopped and looked back. "You're so young, at times, Bill. Irene is for laughs, but the young one! And you could so easily have slipped over the edge, that time you had pneumonia. I'd have inherited the business. *I'd* have been the big shot."

"You are the big shot," Bill said coldly. "I've never known a girl to give me a second look when you're around."

Eliot sighed, murmured, "I cannot argue against fact," and departed.

Bill followed him to the front door and had started to close it after him when he heard footsteps. He stopped and peered down the steps with a vaguely puzzled expression.

They were the footsteps of a person who limped.

Chapter Three

BILL SAW THE HAT WITH THE CHERRIES PASS BY AND MOVE on down towards the corner. He closed the door and reflected that for a woman who limped, she certainly kept going. Probably lived in the neighborhood, although he couldn't seem to place her.

He went to the telephone and put an advertisement for a housekeeper in the morning's paper. Mrs. Goodhue had walked out on him before this and he fully expected that she'd be back, but this time he intended to teach her a lesson. She'd find someone installed when she returned, using her room. Well, no, he wouldn't be spiteful. He could fix the other room up there, but the newcomer would be using Mrs. Goodhue's bathroom. That ought to get her goat.

He went up to his room and wandered over to the mirror. His hair was sticking up again. He had almost black hair, with a wave, and the wave seemed to have moved up into a curl. Well, it seemed to be the style, now, for men to have a tuft of hair brushed up over the forehead, but he didn't like it. He brushed it down firmly, and then went off to take a shower.

On the way back from the bathroom, he knocked on Irene's door, and she called, "Yes?"

"What shall I wear tonight, Mother?"

She came to the door, wrapped in a robe that seemed to be made of pure gold, and laughed while she shook her head at him. "You must *not* call me Mother, not ever. A great hulking brute of a thing like you!"

"All right, but answer my question. I know the sort of costume you'll be wearing when you descend the stairs, attired for this simple evening meal, so what would you advise me to wear?"

18

"Black tie, darling. We positively are not going to be fancy tonight."

Bill dressed and was conscious, on the way downstairs, of an ebbing of his feeling of well-being. He didn't want to go out. He was hungry already, and it would be hours before he got anything to eat. Madeleine bothered him, too. She'd bullied him when they were small, and now that he was bigger and stronger than she was, she'd developed something else. Something that forced him to go out to dinner with her. He didn't want to get entangled with Irene in any way; it simply wasn't his kind of life. Going out endlessly for meals, drinking, dancing, dressing up—and being completely whacked the next day. Well, he'd see that they came back early tonight.

A series of chords from the piano in the parlor startled him, and he went to the archway and looked in. It was Madeleine, wearing a green dress now, with very short sleeves, but still nothing that sparkled.

She looked up at him and dropped her hands into her lap. "I'm afraid your piano is very much out of tune."

He walked in and said, "Nobody ever plays it. As a matter of fact, you were the last one. You used to practice on it. The noise was awful."

Madeleine stood up. "I can't play it. Just as well, apparently."

"Not at all. I'll have it tuned tomorrow. Is your mother within hailing distance of being ready?"

"I don't know." She lit a cigarette, and wandered over to the window. "Here comes that loudmouth, your friend Eliot."

Bill laughed shortly. "He isn't my friend, he's my cousin."

Irene started down the stairs as Eliot rang at the front door. She looked gorgeous, and was informed of this fact by Eliot, who presently turned to Madeleine and told her that she looked lovely.

"Let's go," Bill said, with a touch of impatience. "I'm hungry, and I don't want to be too late getting home. I'm a dull boy who likes work."

Irene laughed at him, but as it happened, he got home at midnight. Madeleine had wanted to come with him, but Irene wouldn't hear of it. She produced a friend to escort her daughter for the rest of the evening, and when Madeleine protested that she couldn't stand his endless stories or the way he twitched his nose, Irene said firmly, "You can't go home alone with Bill, dear. It simply would not do. If Mrs. Goodhue were there, of course it would be all right, but you see, she isn't."

Bill went straight to bed and to sleep. He got up to absolute silence the following morning, and after dressing, went along to the corner drugstore for his breakfast. He glanced through the paper and nodded with satisfaction when he found his advertisement there.

Eliot did not show up at the office until after ten, and to Bill's frown he said, "You might as well erase that boss look from your face because you know perfectly well that I was not out on business of my own last night. You went home and got *your* sleep and left me holding the bag. There are times, you know, when we worms will turn."

"A team of draught horses couldn't have dragged you home last night when I went. Now that you're here, for God's sake go and do some work."

Irene phoned at noon. "Bill, dear, three women have been here about the housekeeping job. Two were impossible, and I hired the other. She's really a dear—pitched right in. Is that all right?"

Bill scowled at the phone, but said with restraint, "Yes, certainly. Quite all right."

"Splendid. Now wait a minute, dear. Don't hang up. Will you take Madeleine to lunch? I have a date and I don't like to leave her dangling here."

"Irene, I'm sorry, but it's quite impossible. I'm up to my ears. I'll take her out tonight."

Irene was pleased. "Oh, tonight would be perfect! I do hate to go off and just leave her sitting around. You *are* a doll, Bill."

Bill put the phone down and sat staring at it absently. Evidently Madeleine didn't have too many dates, and yet she was beautiful. But her personality was quite different from Irene's.

He picked up a letter and then put it down again. Why, Madeleine was twenty-nine, and Irene must have been married at least twice when she'd been that age. No wonder she was a bit worried about her daughter. Not only was she still unmarried, but she apparently had no occupation.

Bill went home fairly early, with Madeleine still vaguely on his mind. Eliot hinted that he'd like to come along, too, although he knew that Bill had a date with Madeleine, since Irene had talked to him on the phone, but he hoped to carry on the evening when Bill took his usual early leave.

Bill said, "Not tonight, son. You can go about your own business, but remember that the office opens at eight-thirty on Monday, and I expect your feet to be under your desk at that hour."

"Yeah." Eliot sighed. "You get to work at eight- thirty. The rest of us merely sit around for an hour trying to wake up. Anyway, nobody expects me here until nine, except you, of course, because I'm the cousin of the boss and owner, and I have pull."

"I'd have fired you yesterday," Bill said briefly, "except for one thing."

"What's that?"

"When you do a bit of work occasionally, it's good."

Eliot settled his tie and murmured, "Well, I know that."

"So when you put in a little more time around here, I'll raise your salary."

"I'd like to be on piecework, paid for what I produce."

"Oh, sure." Bill nodded. "I can well imagine all the places you'd be interviewing people and promoting good will for the firm. You'd have to carry the funds for your expense account around in a satchel."

"Well," Eliot said wistfully, "no harm trying."

"None at all."

Bill expected the usual noise and laughter when he got home, but the house was very quiet. He could hear someone moving around on the basement floor, and supposed that it was the new housekeeper hired by Irene. He brought the paper in from the front steps and sat down in the hall to read, figuring that in this position he'd be bound to run across one or the other of his guests, and so find out whether or not he was supposed to dress again tonight. He hoped it wouldn't be necessary, since Madeleine was not exactly like her mother.

He became interested in an article and did not hear Irene's light step as she descended the stairs.

She cried, "Darling! Is this the most comfortable place you can find to read your paper?"

"No, but I wanted to be sure and see you on your way out. You always look so ravishing."

Irene laughed and spun around, and her coral colored skirt fluttered softly while Bill received a whiff of an exotic scent.

He smiled and asked, "How do you get so many dates, all willing to dress up when they take you out?"

Irene dropped a light kiss on his forehead. "It would be a hard thing to explain to a dear, plodding soul like yourself. I'm attractive, but I help things along a little, too."

Bill nodded. "Madeleine's different, I guess."

Irene frowned and shrugged. "She's so beautiful, but perhaps she isn't silly enough. I'll admit she hasn't many dates, and she won't let me make any for her. I've really done my best, but she's just stubborn."

"Is she coming out with me tonight?"

Irene gave her head an impatient little shake. "I'm afraid not. I suppose I should have phoned you. She claims a slight headache, or something. Actually, she was simply infuriated with me."

Bill discovered that he was disappointed. He said rather severely, "You shouldn't try to wangle dates for he. It's probably the reason she doesn't have any—makes people think she can't get them."

"Oh, yes, of course you're right." Irene heaved a vast sigh. "Really—that girl! The trouble she's been to me."

Bill wanted to question that, but Irene's date turned up and claimed her.

When they had gone, Bill stood in the hall debating as to whether he should go upstairs and try to urge Madeleine to come out with him. As he hesitated, someone came along the hall from the back of the house, and he felt the hair prickling on his scalp as he recognized the limp.

Chapter Four

SHE CAME INTO THE FRONT HALL SMILING AND WITH AN apron tied neatly about her waist. She appeared to be the same woman he had seen on the subway, but without the cherries, he could not be sure. The walk seemed to be the same, but any limp was just a limp, after all—and what did it matter, in any case?

"Mr. Runson," she said quietly. "Mrs. Wisner hired me this morning, but told me that of course you'd have to confirm it. I have my references here." She fumbled in a pocket and drew forth several envelopes. "My name is Mrs. Reilly."

Bill accepted the envelopes, and said, "Thank you, Mrs. Reilly. I'll look over the references and give them back to you. I'm sure you'll be very satisfactory."

She looked competent and respectable, and he would not have bothered with the references except for the incident of the day before. He asked, "Do you live in the neighborhood?"

"Oh, no. My home is in Brooklyn."

He was surprised. Brooklyn was a good distance away, so what could have been her business around this area yesterday? Unless she and the cherried hat were two different people.

"You have a home in Brooklyn?" he asked.

She nodded. "Just a small apartment. It belongs to my son. I stay with him when I'm not working."

"I see, yes. Did Mrs. Wisner show you your room?"

"No, she said I would have to wait until you came home."

"I'll take you." He started up the stairs, and then, remembering the limp, he stopped. "There's a room on the third floor, but perhaps you'd prefer the one in the basement. It's beside the dining room and opens from the kitchen, and it has a window that looks onto the garden at the back."

"Oh, yes." She smiled. "That would be fine. I'd love that room."

"I don't think it's damp," Bill said, "but it is a bit small. The one on the third floor is nicer."

"No, no. I saw the little room. I'd like it *much* better."

They went down to the basement floor, and after they had looked the room over, she asked about dinner.

"I usually have dinner at home," Bill said. "Mrs. Wisner is out, tonight, but I believe her daughter will be in."

"Miss Smith?"

Bill looked into space. Smith? Yes, that was Madeleine's name, but how could Irene ever have brought herself to marry a Smith? It had been her first marriage, of course, when she'd been young and inexperienced.

Mrs. Reilly shook her head. "*She* won't be in for dinner. She's going out. She told me so."

"But her mother said—I mean, I think she has a slight head-ache, or something. Look, you'd better wait until I go up and check."

Mrs. Reilly smiled at him, and he found himself smiling back. He reflected as he went off that she really seemed a very nice person.

He got as far as the front hall upstairs and then stopped with his jaw sagging.

Madeleine was coming down the stairs, and he had to look twice before he was sure of her identity. Her hair was arranged on the top of her head with a bandeau of brilliants to hold it in place, and she wore a pink satin dress that was studded with tiny stones which sparkled and flashed fire in the light. The skirt was slit to the knee on one side. A white fur lay over her shoulder, and her face was heavily made up. She caught sight of Bill as she reached the bottom and started violently.

"Oh!"

Bill thought that her eyes looked dark blue now, instead of gray. He cleared his throat. "I, er, understood you had a slight headache."

She pulled the white fur cape around her neck and murmured, "No, it's—it's better."

"Are we going out, then?"

"Oh, no," she said quickly. "I didn't think you'd take Mother's vulgar arrangements seriously. Didn't she phone you? I told her to let you know that you were off the hook."

"It didn't feel like a hook," Bill said mildly. "In fact, I'd have liked it. You have another date?"

"Yes, I—I've had this date for some time. Mother knew about it, but she has a head like a piece of Swiss cheese."

"Well—" Bill smiled wryly. "I think I'll go off somewhere and sulk. Last night, when you went out with me, you were more or less dressed in sackcloth and ashes, and look at you now."

She laughed. "Mother taught me to dress to the personality of my date."

"Which seems to suggest that I'm a very dull boy indeed."

There was a knock on the front door, and Madeleine moved forward quickly. "That's my taxi."

"Do you mean to tell me that your date is such a boor that he doesn't come around to pick you up?"

She slid him a look from eyes that still seemed to be dark blue and laughed a little. "He's an enemy of yours. He really couldn't set foot in this house."

She went out and closed the door behind her, and Bill walked over and opened it again. He watched her cross the sidewalk and get into the taxi, while a woman walking a dog stopped and stared. There was no one else in the taxi.

Bill glanced at his watch and saw that it was seven o'clock. The September evening was still light, but tomorrow the clocks would go back an hour, and the dark would come earlier. Tomorrow was Sunday, and he could rest. Eliot always griped about working on Saturdays, but they had to at this time of the year. Later it would be only Saturday morning, and during the summer months they did not work on Saturday at all. But nothing satisfied Eliot.

He turned away and went towards the kitchen, and found himself wishing that he'd picked up another cab and followed

Madeleine. He asked Mrs. Reilly to get him something to eat, and then had to return to answer another ring at the front door.

It was Eliot, clean and shining from head to toe. Bill looked him up and down, and said, "You're a bit late, fella. They've both gone out."

"On a Saturday night? But, how crude."

"What's crude about going out on Saturday night?"

"Everything," Eliot murmured. "Among those in the know. I'm fashionable and I'd have gone away for the weekend, save for the fact that you are housing two such resplendent dolls."

"Did you have an invitation for the weekend?"

"Well, no. It's just one of those drop-in-sometime affairs. I'm afraid you'll have to sneak out to the delicatessen and get some more bread and a few cold cuts."

"Are you trying to say that you want to stay here, tonight?"

"Yes."

Bill stared at him. "You want me to have an extra bed made up for you, when you live only a few blocks away?"

"I'm very much in demand," Eliot sighed. "I go away every weekend until well into November, so I allow a fellow the use of my apartment on Saturday nights. He comes to town every week-end *from* the country. Odd, isn't it?"

Bill let the door swing wider and said resignedly, "All right, come in. I suppose you pick up a bit of extra change that way."

Eliot moved gracefully into the hall. "I brought my own sheets and towels so that your laundry bill need not be affected."

"Good. Where's my present?"

"Eh?"

"I've seen you buy presents to take out to your weekend hosts and hostesses. Where's mine?"

"Ah, yes. Well, do get something you really like with the money you'll save on the laundry."

"Have you had your dinner?" Bill demanded.

"My dear fellow, it is only a little after seven. Of course I've not had dinner."

"Go in and make yourself a cocktail," Bill said, "or whatever foul drink you pour down your throat at this hour. I'll go and tell

Mrs. Reilly to put on another potato."

Eliot muttered, "Potato!" and made a face, and Bill went on down to the kitchen.

Mrs. Reilly was singing softly to herself, and she was quite amiable about setting another place for dinner. She said, "That's nice. Now you'll have company," and added, "Mr. Runson, could you move the bed in my room a little away from the window? I tried, but it's too heavy for me."

Bill nodded and went into the little bedroom. He moved the bed and was on his way out before he saw the hat on the bureau. It was the hat with the cherries.

Chapter Five

SO SHE WAS THE SAME WOMAN, BILL STOOD FOR A MOMENT, thinking it over. There was no doubt but that she had been startled when she'd seen him on the subway, and she had followed him when he'd left the train. She'd been behind him on the street, and quite a bit later, she'd walked past the door. And now she was in his house.

It could still be coincidence, of course. She might have followed him up the street because she had an appointment with someone living in that direction and was simply returning from it when he saw her later. Then she had seen his ad and had applied for the position. But why had she been startled when she saw him on the subway?

He went into the kitchen. She was busy at the stove, and he hesitated for a moment and then said, "Mrs. Reilly, you seem familiar to me. Have we met before at any time?"

He was more puzzled than ever when her whole face lit up.

"You mean, you think you know me?"

"Well, I—I'm not sure. I saw you on the subway, yesterday, and then on the street. Perhaps it's just that."

Her expression changed a little. "Oh, yes. I saw you, too. I sort of think maybe I've met you somewhere before, but I don't know where."

She turned back to the stove, and Bill stood in indecision. He had an impression that she'd been about to tell him something and had changed her mind.

"Will you call your friend?" she said presently. "I'm putting dinner on right away."

Bill went upstairs and found Eliot reading the paper with a glass at his elbow.

"Come on. Dinner."

"Ah? Then I shall drain my glass and be with you at once."

There was little conversation at the table except that which was supplied by Mrs. Reilly, who had something to say each time she came in from the kitchen to attend to them. She paid little heed to Eliot, although Bill had taken him to the kitchen to introduce them, but she was alert to anticipate Bill's every want, until Eliot was forced to comment.

"Long live the king."

"It's a new broom sweeping clean," Bill said. "In a few days she'll be snatching my plate away before I'm finished."

"Like Mrs. Goodhue."

"Only when she was in a hurry," Bill protested.

"Not only when she was in a hurry. Many was the time when I had no saucer to return my cup to. I got so much in the habit of holding on to my saucer when I raised my cup for a sip, that I was embarrassed to find myself doing it in respectable places."

"You're so self-centered," Bill said, "that it wouldn't occur to you that she might want to get cleared away in order to have some time to herself. What did you want with a saucer, anyway? You ought to learn not to slop your coffee out of the cup."

"I am being unreasonable, of course," Eliot said gracefully. "Next time I shall tell her simply to put the spoon in the cup."

Bill frowned. "I don't know about next time. She can stay away as long as she pleases, and she's going to find it hard to get back."

When they had finished dinner, they complimented Mrs. Reilly on her cooking, and Eliot asked if she would make a bed up for him.

"You'll make up your own bed," Bill said firmly. "Mrs. Reilly is a little lame and she's not to climb up to the third floor. I have a weekly cleaning woman who can attend to things up there."

Mrs. Reilly beamed at him. "That's real nice of you, not to expect me to do too much climbing. It's my hip, you know."

Bill went upstairs with Eliot and helped him to make up the bed in the room next to Mrs. Goodhue's. When they had finished, Eliot went into Mrs. Goodhue's room, and Bill called after him, "What are you doing in there?"

"Just curious. I want to find out how much she's left." He turned on the light and looked in the closet and opened a couple of drawers. "See? It's just as I thought she's taken no more than a nightie. It's a depressing thought, but I'm afraid she's coming back."

"What makes you think I'll take her back?"

"Of course you will. She has the evil eye on you, and you're afraid of her."

"May I ask," said an icy voice, "what you are doing in my room?"

Eliot turned and fled basely, but Bill put his chin up and headed into it.

"I'm inspecting the room preparatory to having it cleaned out. I understood that you had left."

"I left," said Mrs. Goodhue, "to hurry to the bedside of my sick sister."

Bill raised his eyebrows. "You told me yesterday that you were leaving if my guests stayed."

Mrs. Goodhue cleared her throat, but she continued to look him in the eye. "You should have told me ahead of time that they were coming. As it was, I quickly made up two rooms for them before I left, and naturally I came back as soon as I could. I'm sure I've never let you down."

Bill regarded the toe of his shoe and said, "Well." He added, "With guests here, and you gone, without any explanation about your sister, I was forced to get someone else in."

She nodded. "It's all right."

Bill said, "I've just hired her, and she's moved in. I can't have her sent away yet. In any case, the guests are still here. You'll just have to work together for a while."

Mrs. Goodhue pulled her chin in towards her neck and folded her lips. "I'll go down and see her at once."

Bill had got as far as the door and he turned and said, "I don't want you to offend her. She's a very nice person. Her name is Mrs. Reilly."

She stared him out of the room, and he found Eliot pressed

against the wall outside.

"What did she do to you?"

"Nothing much," Bill said airily. "It was more in the form of a warning."

They went downstairs to the library behind the parlor, and Bill sat down with a book while Eliot poured two highballs.

"Have you enough liquor for the weekend?"

Bill had opened his book and made no answer, and Eliot brought the glasses and put one down beside him. "It's very rude to sit reading in front of a guest."

Bill lowered the book and picked up the highball. "You seem to be in low water. Has it actually come to the point where I'm your only company for the evening?"

Eliot sighed. "These things happen occasionally even to the most sought after man-about-town, but I'll make you do until the girls get back."

"You'd better get a book to tide you over the time between when I go to bed and the girls get back."

"Certainly not. The least you can do as a host is to stay up and amuse me."

The front door knocker began a quiet, persistent tapping, and Bill got up to go and answer it. Eliot wandered after him, shaking his head. "Two serving women in the house, and yet you are obliged to answer doors yourself."

"It's easy to see that you have no serving women at all," Bill retorted. "Today, it would be considered downright uncouth for me to expect either of those ladies to tramp up and down stairs, answering doors."

Eliot murmured, "Of course. But who could be at *your* door at this hour? A courteous burglar, perhaps."

Bill opened the door, and confronted a slight young man who was carrying a suitcase.

"Pardon me, but is this the Runson residence?"

Bill nodded.

"I believe my mother, Mrs. Reilly, was hired as housekeeper today? I have her suitcase."

"Oh, yes." Bill opened the door wider. "Come in."

The man stepped into the lighted hall, put the suitcase down, and then looked up at Bill.

His face went gray and his knees began to buckle, and Bill caught him just before he slid to the floor.

Chapter Six

BILL EASED THE LIMP BODY ONTO A SEAT UNDER THE STAIR railings and then glanced up at Eliot.

Eliot was standing very still, with his mouth sagging a little, and the only movement about him was the smoke drifting up from his cigarette.

"Well, come on!" Bill said impatiently. "Do you think you're the Statue of Liberty? Run down and get his mother, and a pail of water."

Eliot departed, still in silence, and Bill tried to arrange his patient more comfortably on the narrow settee.

Mrs. Reilly presently appeared, panting a little, and crouched down beside her son. She stroked his hair and said gently, "Joe … come, now … it's all right … you must open your eyes."

Joe moved his head and his breath went out in a long mutter.

"He'll be all right now," Mrs. Reilly said. "He's subject to these fainting spells—has them every once in a while. I think it would be better if you left me alone with him, so he doesn't get all upset when he comes out of it."

Bill and Eliot retreated, and Bill called back, "He'd better stay here for the night. Let us know if we can help you with him."

They went to the library, and Eliot looked down at the pail of water which he still carried in his hand. "What did you want this for, anyway?" he demanded aggrievedly. "Mrs. Goodhue was there when I got it, and she sneered fiercely and said it wouldn't be necessary. I'll have to get rid of the water before I take it back or she'll crow over me disgustingly."

"Why don't you drink it?"

Eliot set the pail on the floor. "No wonder the poor fellow fainted when he looked at you. Your hair was enough to scare him. Don't you know that the fancy pompadour style simply doesn't go with your homespun face?"

Bill walked to a mirror and frowned into it. That front piece of hair always stood up in a curl if he didn't paste it down with lotion, and for the last couple of days he hadn't been able to make it stay down at all. He ran an uneasy hand through it and then turned back to Eliot in a sudden temper.

"You have a damned nerve to be criticizing my hair. That pile of stuff on your skull looks as though it had been swept up with a dustpan and broom. You remind me of Louis XV."

"I am supposed to remind you of Louis XV," Eliot said imperturbably. "My barber spends a great deal of time over the fashioning of my hair. I am of the smart set and I must be dressed and coiffured correctly, but you are a solid business man, and that black curl standing up in the middle of your forehead is as silly as hell."

Bill had stopped listening and he murmured, "Where can the fellow sleep if he stays here?"

"You should have a larger house—all your money."

"Yes, of course, so that more people could stay with me."

"Only three rooms on the second floor, and one bath." Eliot shook his head. "Three rooms on the third floor, and one bath. Which reminds me. Could it be possible that I must share the facilities up there with that human cactus?"

"What human cactus?"

"Goodhue."

Bill yawned and shook his head. "You'll have to sleep with me tonight."

Eliot shuddered and glanced at the bucket of water. "Do you mean that I have to share that hideous double bed with you? I think I'm going to swoon."

"Go ahead."

"But what about the third room upstairs?"

"Storage," Bill said. "Has been ever since servants became rare and precious."

"But, listen. Wait a minute." Eliot dropped his voice and glanced over his shoulder. "What about my sheets? They're on that bed. You can't put the fellow on my sheets."

Bill was heading towards the hall, and he said indifferently, "Serve you right for getting funny and bringing them over."

He found Joe sitting up and sipping pallidly at a cup of tea while Mrs. Reilly and Mrs. Goodhue watched him from two adjacent chairs.

Mrs. Reilly stood up and murmured, "He's better now."

Bill nodded. "He'd better stay here for the night. It would be too long a trip for him back to Brooklyn. There's a room already prepared. Mr. Runson was going to use it, but he can bunk in with me."

Mrs. Reilly smiled nicely, but Mrs. Goodhue stirred and said dourly, "He could take a cab."

"No." Bill glanced at her. "I understand he lives alone. It's better this way."

Joe looked up. "Do you think I should stay, Mother?"

"Yes, dear."

Joe stood up, and Bill took his arm. "We'll take the stairs slowly."

Eliot followed them all the way to what was to have been his room and stood in the doorway thinking of his sheets and wishing that he hadn't been quite so funny.

Joe said, "I guess I'll have to sleep in my underwear."

Bill glanced around the room, and his eye fell on Eliot's small overnight bag. "Not at all," he said cheerfully. "There'll be a pair of pajamas here, exquisitely laundered and possibly scented with some tweedy perfume." He opened the bag, and after a moment's searching, pulled out two garments of royal blue silk, beautifully tailored, and the jacket elaborately monogrammed. "Here you are. They'll be nice and soft against your skin. And slippers to match."

Eliot let out a yell, which was quickly muffled as Bill pushed him out into the hall and closed the door behind them. "Shut up, and don't be so stingy—frail, sick boy like that. I'll lend you some pajamas."

"You mean," Eliot said coldly, "those striped, laundry-bag sort of things that you buy in the bargain basements."

"I don't buy them in bargain basements. They are left over from my father. He ordered them by the dozen, every twenty-five years."

Eliot started down the stairs and muttered, "I'll be even with you for this."

"We *are* even. I've been getting even with you."

They found Irene in the front hall, sitting on the chair recently occupied by Mrs. Goodhue. She was alone and her head drooped a little. She gave them only a faint smile.

"Darling!" Eliot said in dismay. "What *has* happened?"

She stood up and twisted her mouth into a charming pout. "It's nothing. I believe I'm tired."

"You're home early," Bill observed.

"Oh, it was only a dinner engagement. I believe I'll go to bed."

"You can't!" Eliot protested. "I came here only to see you, and now you want to leave me."

"We-ll—" She smiled at him. "One very small, weak drink, perhaps."

Bill followed them into the parlor, and Eliot cheerfully set about making drinks. He had to go down to the kitchen for ice, but paused long enough to tell Bill that it was pretty crude not to have a small refrigerator installed somewhere on the main floor.

When he had gone, Bill asked, "Are you worried about something, Irene?"

She shook her head and said quickly, "No, no."

"Madeleine went out with some other fellow. You see, she's a big girl now, and you shouldn't be making her dates for her."

Irene made an impatient gesture with her hand. "Of course. I know that. But I—well, frankly, I don't like this—this fellow, and I wanted to get her interested in someone else. You, perhaps."

"Me?"

"Yes."

"What about Eliot?"

"Oh, *no!*"

"Why not?"

"He's—well, he's mine." She laughed suddenly for the first time.

"You don't think Eliot would make a good husband for a girl?"

Irene extended the toe of a glittering slipper and smiled down at it. "Bill, dear, no mother wants her daughter to marry a play-boy."

"Still—" Bill put a match to a cigarette and shook his head a little. "A good many of these playboys have turned into success-ful husbands."

"Oh, you're quite right, of course," Irene said petulantly. "I always thought it better to marry the solid citizens, and now, you see, I'm sorry. The playboys are so much more fun. Of course, I *did* make good money out of it."

Bill looked up at her. "I thought you were broke?"

She glanced at her slipper again and drew a long breath. "No," she said, "I'm not broke. I'm just desperate."

"What's the trouble?"

Irene compressed her lips, and there was a silence. Bill found himself looking at a square space on the wall where it was evi-dent that some picture had been hanging. He puzzled over it ab-stractedly until he remembered that it had been an expensive oil portrait of himself.

Chapter Seven

BILL FROWNED AND GOT QUICKLY OUT OF HIS CHAIR. THE Reilly woman. Who else could have taken it?

Irene asked, "What is it? What's the matter?" but he hurried off without hearing her.

Downstairs, Eliot was coming out of the kitchen with a bowl of ice, and when Bill brushed past him and went to Mrs. Reilly's door, he stopped and watched with one eyebrow elevated.

Bill had to knock several times before Mrs. Reilly called sleepily, "Yes? What is it?"

Bill cleared his throat. "There's an oil painting missing from upstairs, a portrait of me when I was younger. Do you know anything about it?"

There was a brief silence, and when Mrs. Reilly spoke, her voice was no longer sleepy. "Oh—oh, yes. Just a minute, please. I brought it down to clean it and then forgot all about it. I—have it in here."

"Would you mind giving it to me?" Bill said firmly. "I want to replace it. You're not to bother with that sort of cleaning. I get someone in at regular intervals to do it."

There was an uneasy interval, and presently the door opened a crack, and the picture was thrust out. The door closed again immediately, and Bill had an uncomfortable idea that Mrs. Reilly was weeping. He called awkwardly, "Thanks. Sorry to have disturbed you. I was afraid the thing was lost, or something."

"Or stolen, or something," Eliot murmured, and rattled the ice in his bowl. "Why are you making such a fuss about that daub? It's a rotten likeness, anyway, except that the so-called artist has that silly curl sticking up on your head. I suppose he couldn't miss it. It's always sticking up. In fact, it's sticking up right now."

Bill ran an agitated hand over his hair and muttered, "I just brushed it down. I've been brushing it down all night. I'll have to change that lousy brand of hair stuff and use pure glue."

They went up together. Bill was silently trying to rid himself of a vague feeling of having been a cad, and Eliot whistled softly.

Upstairs, Bill went over and hung the portrait and then stood looking at it for a moment. He realized that he didn't like it much, but his father had had it done shortly before his death and had thought a lot of it.

Irene was standing at the front window, peering out between the lace curtains, and she turned as Eliot brought her a drink. He smiled at her. "Watching for the return of your erring daughter?"

"No." She moved over to a small love seat. "I don't expect Madeleine for ages. I was just dreaming."

Bill looked at her. She seemed thoroughly depressed, and he remembered what she'd said earlier. Desperate.

"What's the matter, Irene?" he asked soberly. "I'd hate to think that you're slopping into the usual parental attitude of worrying about your child all the time, no matter what the situation. It isn't like you."

Irene shrugged. "If there's one thing in which I'm thoroughly experienced, it's men. I know them, and I know the differences in them. So I have to sit by, helpless, and watch my only daughter walk straight into misery and disaster. I've done what I could. She has beauty, but she's a bit serious and hasn't gone out with a great variety of boys. If she had, she'd have thrown this one aside without a second look. *Can't* you two rush her, most violently? It might turn her head, and perhaps she'd forget *him*."

"But that would be delightful," Eliot said. "Such a charming girl."

"Oh, charming." Irene sounded bitter. "Of course. But she—well, she's had good chances, but she turned them all down."

"Chances at what?" Bill asked.

"At a good marriage. What else?"

"What about a career, or work of some sort? Isn't she interested in anything?"

Irene frowned, and her face closed a little.

Eliot asked Bill, "Do you think a woman should go in for a career other than marriage?"

"Don't be a silly ass," Bill said mildly. "In this day and age the woman who thinks only of marriage is a fool. It's what makes for rotten marriages."

"Most interesting," Eliot murmured. "If a little acid."

"Well—" Bill stood up. "I wouldn't marry any woman who didn't earn her own living one way or another."

Eliot looked down into his glass, swallowed a yawn, and murmured, "Cheap."

Irene was smiling again and seemed to have cast off her depression. "I must have something to eat. I've had too many drinks."

It developed that Eliot was the only one of the three who knew anything about the preparation of food, and he presently went down to the kitchen alone. Irene wanted them all to go until Bill remembered that Mrs. Reilly was sleeping in the next room and should not be disturbed.

When Eliot had left, Irene wandered over to the window again and peered out.

"If you don't expect Madeleine this early, why do you keep looking for her?"

She turned away abruptly and took a cigarette from a box on the table. "Oh, I don't know. I suppose I keep hoping she's fought with him, or something."

Bill nodded and then glanced at the clock. "I don't believe I want anything to eat. I think I'll go to bed."

"No, please. You don't need to reduce, and a snack will do you good. So you believe that all women should earn their own livings?"

"Certainly. I'm very much against training that forces them to think only of men. They should have an interest outside of romance, as men do."

"Well—" Irene smiled at him. "Perhaps you're right. Of course

Madeleine is interested in her music, too much so, I sometimes think. After all, she's twenty-two now, and not even engaged, and I was married when I was eighteen."

"Good for you," Bill said dryly. "But I'm a little confused. Madeleine seems to have dallied about her growing up. When we were children, she was only two years younger than I was, and now I'm nearly thirty-one and she's trailing along at twenty-two."

"Be quiet, will you!" Irene said sharply. "Haven't you any tact?"

"Madeleine didn't look any twenty-two when she went out to-night."

"She let you see her?"

"She didn't make a point of it. I happened to come into the hall as she was going out."

Irene put out her cigarette with savage little jabs. "She looks awful that way, doesn't she?"

Bill shook his head. "I wouldn't say awful. Certainly I like her more restrained type of dressing much better, but she looked fairly lavish."

"It doesn't suit her."

"But you dress that way, to a point, at least."

"Oh, Bill, darling!" Irene made an impatient little gesture. "I'm older, and in my day it was different. She's smart and she has beauty. She has no need … It's that fool, Inavsy."

Bill raised his eyebrows. "Inavsy?"

She nodded and stared at the carpet with her lips compressed.

"Hasn't he another name that comes before or after?"

Irene gave a delicate snort. "If you were to ask him what his other name is, I expect he'd say, 'the Great.' "

Bill laughed, but Irene continued to frown. Eliot appeared at the door and said aggrievedly, "You'll have to come down to the dining room for the snack. The dumbwaiter isn't working."

Bill stood up. "What's wrong with it?"

"I don't know, but if you start to fix it now, I'll scream, and that's not an idle threat."

Irene laughed and slipped her hand through Eliot's arm. "You're a perfect love. I adore you."

They went down to the dining room where Eliot had laid out

the snack. It looked artistic and tasty, and Irene gave a little coo of pleasure.

"My mother was disappointed at having no daughter," Eliot said, "so she brought me up as a girl, since I was the prettiest of her boys."

"There's not a word of truth in that," Bill said to Irene. "He always loved food and was fascinated by the cooking of it. His mother was a famous cook, and she was always asking him for God's sake to get out from under her feet when she was in the kitchen. Anyway, this coffee is lousy."

Eliot sipped tentatively and frowned. "I believe you're right. There *is* a peculiar taste to it, but I'd guess that the trouble is in your coffeepot. Sloppy cleaning by Mrs. Reilly, probably. Goodhue, the iron woman, would never turn out a job like that."

"Don't bicker, darlings," Irene said contentedly. "The coffee is perfectly all right, and the sandwiches are wonderful."

A voice from the door asked, "May I have some, too?" and they turned to see Madeleine there. She had removed the band from her head, and her hair was around her face again.

Eliot and Bill stood up, and Eliot escorted her to a seat at the table and supplied her with a cup and saucer. Bill just stood where he was, and reflected on the state of his emotions. He was gone on this girl, no doubt about it. Falling right in with Irene's plans. And his rival was a villain by the name of Inavsy.

Irene gestured at him. "Sit down, Bill, do." She turned to Madeleine and added, "Did you have a good time, dear?"

"Oh, yes, very—I mean, I had a very good time."

Irene's eyes lingered on her for a moment, and then she said, "That's nice, dear. Eliot, do make some more of these delightful sandwiches."

Bill broke up the party at a little after two by announcing, simply, that he was going to bed, and the rest decided to follow him.

In Bill's bedroom, Eliot broke out into grumbling when he was presented with a pair of pajamas which had belonged longed to his host's father. He muttered, "I notice that you don't wear them."

"Yes, I do. Mine are a different color, that's all. I like them."

Eliot gingerly crawled into the double bed and moaned, "This is ghastly. I shan't be able to sleep all night. I never can sleep in the same bed with anyone else."

"Shut up," Bill said drowsily. "Go and sleep on the floor."

Bill slept heavily and late, and it was ten o'clock before he flung back the covers and rolled out. Eliot was still asleep, with his mouth open, and Bill gave him a fleeting grin and then wandered over to the bureau and peered at his reflection.

He stood there for a long time, staring with dropped jaw. The black curl on the front of his head had been cut off at the scalp, and he didn't look like himself at all.

Chapter Eight

BILL FINGERED THE CROPPED PLACE ON HIS SKULL, WHICH was all that was left of his curl, and was possessed by a sudden fury. He stalked over to the bed and put one hand on Eliot's head and the other under his chin and closed the gaping mouth.

Thus shut off from air, Eliot woke up and began to struggle, and Bill eventually let go, short of murder. He demanded unreasonably, "What's the matter with you? Don't you ever use your nose for breathing?"

Eliot was busy replacing oxygen in his system, and Bill added ominously, "You've gone too far, this time."

Eliot gasped, in utter outrage, "*I've* gone too far!"

"Well—look at me! And stop those silly antics."

"I can't look at you, not before breakfast. Trying to strangle me in my sleep! Sometimes I think you ought to be certified."

"After you," Bill said grimly. "Now, I'm warning you, I'm not putting up with your stupid pranks any longer. If you had to get funny and cut the damned thing off you could at least have left enough for the barber to work on. And this is Sunday, too, no barbers open. I'll have to go around all day looking as though the moths had been at me."

"Your curl!" Eliot got up from the side of the bed where he had been sitting and went over to where Bill was peering once more into the mirror. "Well! Quite an improvement, really."

"I'll be damned if you're going to get away with this," Bill muttered.

"*Me? I* had nothing to do with it. I'm too occupied with my

44

own affairs to care what sort of a silly ass you look like."

"So you say, but I know you had a hand in this, and you can pack up and leave."

Eliot looked at him for a moment. "You really think I did it, which means that you didn't do it yourself. Yes, I shall leave. I couldn't sleep anyway knowing that some demented ghoul is creeping around the house at night with a pair of shears."

"Nuts," Bill said composedly. "How do you suppose anybody could come in here and cut off a piece of my hair without waking me? I'm not a particularly heavy sleeper."

"No." Eliot hunched his shoulders. "Nor am I. I'd have wakened, too. So what right have you to accuse me? I couldn't have cropped your thick skull without waking you."

It was a good point, and Bill found no answer.

"Perhaps you're a somnambulist," Eliot said thoughtfully. "That curl has been lying heavily on your subconscious, and you had to get rid of it while your conscious mind was asleep."

Bill laughed shortly. "I've never walked in my sleep since the day I was born."

"You can't know that, and anyway, there's always a first time."

"No, there isn't," Bill said decidedly. "Not for me. I slept very well last night. Went out like a light, and the last thing I heard you say was that you couldn't sleep with anybody and would be awake all night. So I suppose you were bored, lying there staring into the darkness, and you idled the time away by cutting off my hair."

"Yes," Eliot said, "how about that? I *can't* sleep with anyone in a double bed, yet last night I went out like a light, too. And don't start telling me it was liquor, because I can't drink comfortably when your eyes are on me. It simply ruins my style. I drank practically nothing last night, and I'm used to a little something. So what put *me* to sleep?"

"I find this a most interesting subject," Bill said coldly. "We really must discuss it at length."

Eliot gave him a thoughtful eye. "Perhaps we'd better. It has just occurred to me that that coffee *did* have a peculiar taste, and when I make coffee it is *always* good. Someone tampered with it while I was upstairs getting you and Irene, which is why we both slept so soundly."

"It's a nice theory." Bill ruffled his shorn head. "Only I find it hard to think of anything more stupid than putting everybody into a sound sleep in order to cut off a lock of my hair."

"There's more to it than that," Eliot said seriously. "We don't know why it was done, but we certainly know how."

Bill walked over and looked into the wastebasket.

"Is it there?"

"No."

"We'd better get dressed," Eliot said. "We'll watch them all most carefully, and the one who shows no astonishment at the sight of you is the one who did the cutting."

Bill nodded, although he was still faintly suspicious of Eliot. But on the other hand, the Reilly woman had behaved in a peculiar manner, first on the subway, then taking his portrait into her room, and her son fainting at the sight of him. Apparently he looked like someone who was connected with them, but surely that was all. He couldn't imagine the woman doping their coffee in order to cut off a piece of his hair.

They went to the bathroom together in order, as Bill put it, to free it more quickly for the women. They showered, scrubbed their teeth, and while Eliot combed his hair into smooth perfection, Bill attempted to paste pieces over his shorn spot with hair oil. Eliot tried to supervise this operation for a while, but eventually gave it up as hopeless and started back towards the bedroom.

He had reached the door when he stopped suddenly and began to wave wildly at Bill, who was following along the hall.

"All right," Bill said composedly, "stop making like a windmill. I'll get there."

Eliot pointed down to the gray carpeting of the hall. "Look! It's a wisp of your stolen hair."

Bill stooped and picked up the fragment. "I guess it is. I suppose your fool theory is correct, then. Must have been Mrs. Reilly who did it. Her bedroom is downstairs, so she'd have had time to put something in the coffee to make sure we'd sleep. But the whole thing seems so absurd."

They dressed quickly, and then Eliot said, "Come on, we'll see if there are any more wisps of hair leading downstairs."

It was so dark on the stairway that Bill had to get a flashlight, and they were about half way down, carefully inspecting the gray carpeting, when Madeleine called from above, "What have you lost?"

She was leaning over the railing in a dark-colored dressing robe, and Eliot looked up and called, "Good morning, angel. How fresh and sweet you look."

"How odd," Madeleine murmured.

And Bill said, "How corny."

Eliot gave him a chilly stare. "How would you know what's corny?"

"He just guesses," Madeleine said, laughing. She started to move away, and then turned back again. "What have you done to your hair, Bill? It looks nice."

"You like it?"

"Yes. I hate pompadours on men—I like the tops of their heads to be fairly flat."

"My dear, I shall run out and get a crew-cut at once," Eliot declared.

"Oh, no. Mother likes pompadours. She likes anything as long as it's in style."

She went off down the hall towards the bathroom, and Eliot turned a slightly anxious look on Bill. "Would you say that she classifies me in with her mother's age group?"

Bill grinned at him. "I thought you were a man of the world. Age has nothing to do with it. It's merely that she automatically groups you with her mother. So would I, and so would you, your-self, for that matter."

"Suppose we look for more hair," Eliot said rather austerely.

They found another wisp on the bottom step of the stairs that led to the basement, and they went on into the kitchen and looked around. The kettle was boiling, coffee was burbling in a percola-tor, and other preparations indicated that there would be wheat cakes and sausages for breakfast.

"Oh, no!" Eliot murmured in a stricken voice.

"What's the matter?" Bill demanded. "It looks better than the boiled eggs Mrs. Goodhue usually serves up."

"My dear fellow, it's so fattening."

Bill looked him over for a moment. "If you were any thinner, I'd shove you in my golf bag along with the other sticks."

Eliot was prowling around the kitchen and he said absently, "Very funny. I never eat fattening things. It pays to be beautiful. Look! Here it is!"

He had opened the lid of a small garbage pail, and Bill went over and peered in. The pail was neatly lined with a brown paper bag and was half full of garbage, and on the top lay Bill's black curl.

They stood looking down together for a moment, and then Eliot glanced quickly around the kitchen. "You see, this is yesterday's garbage. The remains of the breakfast isn't in yet. She's had hers, but it's still lying around. It's Mrs. Reilly, all right. Goodhue gets her garbage put away immediately."

"What do you mean?"

"I mean that it's Mrs. Reilly who's getting the breakfast."

Mrs. Reilly appeared at that moment and gave them a cheerful smile. "Are you gentlemen ready—" She stopped suddenly, and her voice rose almost to a shriek. "Oh! Oh, no!"

She was staring at Bill's shorn head.

Chapter Nine

MRS. REILLY STOOD WITH HER SORROWING EYES ON BILL'S head until he became irritated and demanded sharply, "What *is* the matter?"

She looked down and began to pat nervously at her apron. "I, er—well, I—I bit my tongue."

"You bit your tongue?"

"Yes, sir. It hurt."

"Oh. Well, I'm sorry."

She turned away to the stove. "I'll have your breakfast ready right away, sir."

"Thank you." Bill glanced at Eliot. "We'll wait in the dining room."

They went off and sat down at the table, and Eliot dropped his voice to a conspiratorial whisper. "You got that, didn't you? It's certain that Mrs. Reilly didn't cut it off. She was very upset at the sight of you. Interesting, eh?"

"Nothing of the sort," Bill said shortly. "It's all very simple. The woman's a bit off her head. I'll have to get rid of her at once. She may be dangerous."

"Oh, no." Eliot's whisper became eager. "You're forgetting that the son fainted at the sight of you, so you look like someone. The son! That's it! *He* cut your hair off. That curl's been sticking up all the time, lately, instead of only weekends. I've noticed it at the office. Hideous, too. Good thing it's gone."

Bill said, "Shut up. I'll get hold of the son and see what I can find out from him."

49

Madeleine came in, and they both stood up. She said, "Sit down, for heaven's sake. I'm not going to join you. Mother's ill, and I want to take something up to her. May I go to the kitchen and arrange for it?"

Bill said, "Of course."

Eliot asked, "Can't I help you? I do hope it's nothing serious?"

"Oh, no—a sort of sick headache, or something. Don't interrupt your breakfast. I can manage perfectly well."

She went on to the kitchen, and they could hear her talking with Mrs. Reilly.

"She really is lovely, isn't she?" Eliot sighed.

Bill nodded. "She didn't say anything more about my hair."

"That," Eliot explained, "is because she rarely notices you at all."

Madeleine did not come back into the dining room, but went through the rear hall with a tray. Bill and Eliot finished breakfast, and Bill left the table and went upstairs. On the second floor, he stopped and listened carefully at Irene's door, but he heard no sound, so he presently straightened up and made for the third floor. Eliot had been following in silence, and on the stairs, Bill turned suddenly and said, "Suppose you go and play somewhere else."

"No. I want to hear what the son has to say. And if you make an issue of it, I'll have an attack of hysterics and spoil all your plans."

Bill muttered "Damn all relatives!" and went on up.

The doors to the rooms occupied by Joe Reilly and Mrs. Goodhue were closed, and Eliot whispered, "Old Ironjaw is taking advantage of the new help and sleeping the day away."

Bill knocked on Joe's door, and it was opened immediately. Joe was neatly dressed and combed and was buttoning the last button on his coat.

"Are you feeling all right again?" Bill asked.

"Oh, yes. Fine. It's just that I'm subject to spells like that one."

"Good. Sit down a minute, will you? I'd like to ask you a question."

Joe perched uneasily on the side of the bed, and Bill took the only chair in the room. Eliot draped himself elegantly against the bureau, and Joe looked quickly from one face to the other with something like fear on his own.

Bill said easily, "I believe I look like someone you and your mother know."

Joe's eyes had fastened onto the top of Bill's head, and Bill raised a hand to try and smooth the side pieces over the gap in the middle.

Joe stood up. "It's been cut off!"

"What's been cut off?" Bill demanded irritably. "What's the matter with you?"

Joe took a deep breath. "I'm glad. Now it will be easier."

"Will you, for God's sake," Bill shouted, "stop horsing around and explain all this nonsense!"

"Yes." Joe sat down again. "What is it you want to know?"

"Do I look like anyone known to you and your mother?"

Joe nodded, and his face was serious. "Yes. You are extremely like my brother, who died last year. My mother has not been able to adjust herself to his death. I don't know where she saw you, or how she got a job with you, but she has been living with me for some time and she has *never* done this type of work before. I want to take her back home with me."

Bill nodded. "Good. My regular housekeeper, Mrs. Goodhue, has come back. I thought she had left, but it seems that there was illness in her family. I'll tell your mother that I shan't need her now, and you can take her back today. I'll pay for a taxi so that you won't have to carry her bag to Brooklyn."

"Thank you," Joe said, "that's very considerate. If you tell her she must leave, it will be easier. I'm sure she'd never come on my say so."

Bill stood up and started towards the door. "I'll attend to it right away."

"What's with the hair business, Joe?" Eliot asked, without moving.

There was a silence, and Bill looked back. "Yes. Why did you say it would be easier with my hair this way?"

"My brother had a piece of hair sticking up in the front, that way. You're still like him, but not so much with that piece of hair gone."

"Did you cut it off?" Eliot asked gently.

Joe stared and swallowed, and Eliot repeated, "Did you cut it off last night while he was sleeping?"

Joe looked from one to the other of them, and said at last, "*I* cut it off?"

"Well, did you?" Bill demanded.

"I don't understand. How could *I* have done such a thing?"

Eliot shifted his position against the bureau. "You could have done it while Mr. Runson was sleeping during the night."

"Ridiculous!" Joe said angrily. "I don't even know this house. I don't know which is Mr. Runson's bedroom."

Bill shrugged. "Let it go. Come on down, and you and your mother can get started."

Joe delayed over some final adjustment to his dressing, and Bill and Eliot went on down.

"There's something more to it than that," Eliot said in a low voice. "Not that I believe he actually did cut your hair off. He seemed to be genuinely astonished."

"Well, what about it?"

"It's funny, that's all. Someone else did it—someone who wanted you *not* to look like Mrs. Reilly's son."

"Ah, nuts!" Bill said. "I know who did it. You."

"*Me?* Are you crazy?"

"No, you are. I always thought there was something wrong with your head, and this proves it. Maybe you did it in your sleep, and you're not going to sleep with me again."

"All right. Go ahead and make everything easy in your lazy mind, no matter how many loose ends are left untied."

"Look," Bill said, "they're leaving today, so why worry about it? They'll be out of the house within an hour."

Mrs. Reilly was inclined to be tearful when informed that her services would no longer be needed, and Bill had to explain about Mrs. Goodhue.

"But she likes me to be here, Mr. Runson. She said so. She said it was too much for one person, and she was glad of the help."

"I've no doubt," Bill said grimly. "Only, I can't afford the two of you."

"Oh, please!" Mrs. Reilly twisted her hands together. "I don't want a salary. I'll do without money. I just want to live here."

Bill shook his head, and after a little further pleading, Mrs. Reilly went to her room and began to drop tears onto her packing.

Bill followed her unhappily. "You know, your son isn't strong, and he really needs you with him to care for him."

She turned her wet eyes on him. "Joe should get married. He's making a good salary, and he should have a wife. I'd rather live somewhere else so that he *can* get married."

"Look," Bill said sensibly, "if you want a job like this, you can get one any day in the week. People are howling for housekeepers."

She went on with her packing without answering, and when Joe came down, Bill phoned for a cab. He and Eliot went out to the curb to see them off, and Bill was relieved to notice that Mrs. Reilly was a little more cheerful. Joe was smiling.

When the cab had rolled off, they went back into the house and met Madeleine in the front hall.

She asked, "Why do you keep water in your bottle of hair lotion?"

Chapter Ten

BILL AND ELIOT LOOKED AT MADELEINE IN A PUZZLED FASHION, and she said to Bill, "Well, why do you?"

Bill shifted his weight from one foot to the other. "Did you say there was water in my bottle of hair oil?"

"Yes, that's what I said." She touched a hand to her hair. "I ran out of my own stuff and saw yours in the bathroom. I have to put a bit of something on my hair, or it won't stay in place, so I used yours. Now, of course, my hair's worse than ever. That's a mean way to trap a person—filling up a bottle with water and leaving it standing there with its label on."

"Is the bottle still in the bathroom?" Bill asked.

"Yes. I felt like smashing it on the floor, only I didn't."

"Ah." Eliot rubbed his hands together. "This thing becomes more interesting all the time. Someone wants him to look like the Reilly boy, someone wants him to be *unlike* the Reilly boy, and each goes to certain lengths to have his way. I told you there was more to it, Bill, but your dull mind thinks that everything is settled simply because you shipped the Reillys out."

"What *are* you talking about?" Madeleine asked curiously.

Bill was already halfway up the stairs, and Eliot said, "Come on, this is becoming absolutely fascinating."

Madeleine allowed him to urge her up the stairs, and they found Bill in the bathroom, sniffing at the bottle of hair oil.

54

"Well?" Eliot demanded.

Bill poured some into the palm of his hand and looked at it. "It's thin, anyway."

"Water is always thin," Madeleine pointed out.

"Taste it," Eliot suggested.

Bill extended his hand. "You taste it. Water mixed with scraps of hair oil shouldn't be too bad, something like one of your special cocktails."

Eliot put his finger gingerly into the little pool in Bill's hand and then sniffed at it carefully.

"Why all the smelling?" Madeleine asked. "I mean, what does water smell like, anyway?"

"There are certain substances that do have odors," Eliot explained loftily. "We are eliminating."

"Suppose I leave it with you, Eliot," Bill said suddenly. "Get a magnifying glass and crawl around until you find out why someone put water in my hair oil and cut off my best piece of hair, and who did it."

"I assume there will be a suitable reward?"

"Eminently suitable," Bill said. "You run along now and start prowling. Madeleine, how about a walk? It's a nice day."

Madeleine stared at him. "A—walk?"

"Your ears," said Eliot, "do not deceive you. He said a walk. And allow me, if I may, to insert a warning. There may come a time when you are so tired and depleted that you agree to marry him—and that would be your weekend diversion. A walk in the park. At other times you would be busy around the house because, of course, with you here, he could dispense with paid service."

"You know, I've half a mind to try it," Madeleine said. "The walk, I mean. I've heard of it, but I've never really done it. Wait until I see whether Mother's still sleeping."

She went along the hall and opened Irene's door a crack, and Bill and Eliot stood and watched her.

"Your man of the world should really try everything," Eliot said thoughtfully. "I believe I'll give this walk business a fling, too."

Bill swung around on him. "Oh, no, you won't. You'll unravel the mystery of my hair, for the reward. This happens to be *my* date."

Eliot raised his shoulders. "All right, keep your plebeian shirt on. But I'll tell you frankly that I don't know how you do it. *I* couldn't organize a date with no financial outlay."

"Don't be absurd," Bill said. "When we get to the park I'll have to buy peanuts, won't I?"

"Ah, yes. I didn't mean to imply that you were cheap, of course."

Madeleine returned, and Eliot followed them down to the front door. He stopped Bill with a hand on his arm and carefully arranged the side pieces of his hair over the gap in the middle. "There, that's better. Try to have a good time, although I'm sure your date would be happier if I were coming, too."

"I would not," Madeleine said. "Mother always told me not to go out with crowds of men until after I'm married."

"I am not a crowd," Eliot called after them.

He watched them out of sight and then went straight to the library for a quick nip, after which he made for the kitchen to get ice for a highball.

The kitchen was in disorder. Nothing had been cleared away, but he merely shrugged and grinned. Not his job, anyway. He got the ice, and paused to admire the refrigerator, which was modern and new and gleaming. The old one stood beside it, and he reflected that Bill would never throw it out—might come in handy for something—save a dime or two somehow. It pulled down the tone of the kitchen, but the kitchen was shabby and old- fashioned, so what was the difference?

He went upstairs, mixed himself a highball, and then proceeded to the second floor. Irene's door was still closed, and he stood outside and listened. He could hear her crying quietly inside, and after a moment's indecision, he went off and then came back, clearing his throat loudly so that she would hear him. He tapped on the door and called, "Irene, are you awake?"

"Eliot?"

"Yes. I wondered if I could mix you a drink. Might help your headache."

There was a short silence, and then she said, "Perhaps it would. Not a martini, a Manhattan."

"Good. I'll be up with it in two shakes."

"No. I'll put on something and come down. I'll feel better if I get up."

He went downstairs and mixed her drink, and she followed presently, wearing a black lace negligee and looking attractively fragile.

"Charming!" Eliot murmured, presenting the cocktail. "Who could possibly know that you're not feeling well?"

She leaned back in her chair and smiled up at him. "Thank you, darling. Where are Madeleine and Bill?"

"They're taking a walk. If you haven't looked out the window yet, it's a nice day."

"A—walk?"

Eliot nodded. "Bill's really throwing all caution to the winds, isn't he? Taking a girl for a walk."

Irene raised her shoulders and let them drop. "It doesn't matter. He's a nice boy."

"Such a responsibility," Eliot said thoughtfully, "getting one's daughter properly married. If she were a boy, you wouldn't have it to worry about."

"I know. Madeleine keeps telling me I don't have it to worry about, anyway. She says for God's sake to let her take care of her own affairs, and if they don't include marriage, that's her business."

"Absurd!" Eliot said. "She *must* get married."

"Of course."

"What about this Inavsy?"

Irene frowned and took a sip of her drink.

"What is his business?" Eliot persisted.

She made an impatient little movement and said, "Oh, nothing," and added immediately, "those two must be taking a long walk. I do wish Bill would become interested in her."

"He is."

"Do you think so?" Irene asked, her face brightening.

He nodded, but her face drooped into a frown again. "That's

only half the battle, of course. What's the use if she won't take an interest in him?"

"She went for a walk with him."

"That's nothing. She's contrary enough to go walking just because it's so dull."

"Yes, perhaps." He shrugged. "She's not one of us."

"No."

There was a short silence, and then Eliot asked, "Did you know that Bill fired Mrs. Reilly this morning?"

"What?"

"Yes. And Mrs. Goodhue is still asleep."

"Then, why in heaven's name," said Irene impatiently, "don't you go and wake her?"

"Not me." Eliot shuddered. "She keeps a little knife always sharpened for me. The kitchen's in a mess, too."

"It can stay that way until she decides to get up." Irene laughed a little. "She has another little knife with my name on it. But why did Bill fire Mrs. Reilly?"

"It seems the son wanted to take her home, partly because Bill looks like her other son, now deceased. I believe that's why she wanted to work here in the first place. Also, Bill lost a lock of his hair sometime during the night."

Irene had opened her mouth to reply when Madeleine and Bill walked in.

"Oh, Mother. You're feeling better?"

Irene nodded, and Eliot promptly told Bill about the state of the kitchen.

Bill frowned. "I'll go up and get Mrs. Goodhue. I suppose she doesn't know that Mrs. Reilly has gone."

He went on up to the third story and knocked smartly at Mrs. Goodhue's door. There was no answer, and after waiting for a while, he turned the knob and peered in. Mrs. Goodhue was not there, and he swung the door wide and walked in, looking about him in a puzzled fashion. The room was very neat, as usual, but the bed was turned down as though she expected to get into it.

Well, perhaps she did. She might be in the bathroom, might be ill …

He searched the third floor and eventually the whole house, but he did not find her. He ended up in the kitchen in a state of irritation that was aggravated by the sight of the mess. He supposed she'd heard Mrs. Reilly leave and had taken off herself. An opened package of bacon and a platter of softening butter lay on the table, and he put them away in the refrigerator and slammed the door. He noticed some metal shelves stacked neatly between the two refrigerators and supposed that they belonged in the old box. He jerked them out, swearing under his breath, and wrenched open the door.

Mrs. Goodhue's body had been wedged into the space left by the shelves.

Chapter Eleven

IRENE, MADELEINE, BILL, AND ELIOT WERE SITTING ABOUT the library in various attitudes of gloom and dejection. Eliot had mixed high-balls for everyone, but the level remained about the same in all the glasses but his own. Irene and Bill were smoking, and Madeleine drummed ceaselessly on the wooden arm of her chair.

"Darling!" Irene said suddenly. "Do go and sit somewhere else! I simply cannot stand that horrid noise. It's like water dripping on my forehead."

Madeleine's fingers became still."Hang on to your nerves, Mother. After all, it isn't the end of everything. It will pass in time."

Irene crushed out a half-smoked cigarette and immediately lighted another one.

Eliot glanced at her. "You really are in a mess, my dear. You must pull yourself together."

"So are you in a mess," Irene snapped. "Your tie is crooked and your front hair has fallen down."

Eliot hastily straightened his tie and molded his hair back into shape with careful hands.

Bill muttered, "How the devil could she have got locked up in that refrigerator? It isn't possible."

Madeleine kicked at the carpet with her toe. "You said that before. Why don't you wait until they come up? They'll tell us what happened."

"Perhaps she wanted to eavesdrop," Eliot suggested, "climbed into the box, and closed it before she realized that she couldn't open it from the inside."

"Don't be an idiot," Madeleine said impatiently. "Nobody could be that stupid, let alone Mrs. Goodhue."

"What's so wrong with that?" Irene demanded. "Mrs. Goodhue adored snooping, and who doesn't, anyway? And that box was a perfect place."

Bill shook his head. "How could she expect to hear anything with the door closed?"

"How do you know she couldn't?" Eliot asked. "Have you ever been inside one?"

"No."

"Now, wait a minute," Irene interrupted. "I think it's possible that she climbed in and left the door slightly open, and then perhaps someone fell against it, or something, and closed it accidentally. She didn't call for help because she didn't want to be found in such a situation—and later, when she discovered she couldn't get out, there was no one around to hear her screams."

A voice from the door said, "That's an interesting theory," and they all turned and stared. The man who stood there was not one of the group who had appeared after Bill's telephone call to the doctor and the doctor's telephone call to the police. He was short and plump and wore a beret on his head.

Bill stood up and asked abruptly, "Who are you?"

"I'm Dykes. I'm in charge of this case, and if you don't mind, I'd like to ask a few questions."

Irene had been viewing the beret. "But surely you are not a policeman?"

"I don't direct traffic, madam. I received a promotion."

"Oh, congratulations," Irene said vaguely. "I suppose you're a plainclothes man. Only I shouldn't think they'd allow you to wear a hat like that."

"We are allowed to wear any plain clothes we choose, madam," Dykes replied distantly.

"Do you call that tie plain?" Eliot asked.

Dykes stared through him with a look he had practiced and perfected some years before, and Eliot wilted and studied a section of the carpet.

Irene seemed unable to take her eyes off the beret. "Don't you take it off in the house? I mean, after all, it *is* a hat."

"Leave us not quibble," Dykes said severely. "I want your names and occupations."

He left Madeleine to the last and bestowed upon her the first smile he had exhibited. It developed that his teeth were yellow and crooked, and she wondered why he hadn't kept them covered. She gave him her name and explained that she was Irene's daughter.

Dykes went so far as to thank her and added, "What is your occupation, if any?"

"Debutante," Irene said firmly.

Madeleine turned on her. "Mother! Please! This is serious. I am a pianist, Mr. Dykes."

"Professional?"

"Yes."

"My daughter has given one or two concerts," Irene interposed, "but it is not necessary for her to work."

"That's nice," Dykes said. "I'd like to be in that spot, myself."

"We're all upset and tired," Bill observed abruptly. "The sooner you get through with us, the better."

Dykes shrugged. "It will take a little time, I'm afraid. Now, I'll have to ask you for a detailed account of your activities yesterday and today."

Irene raised her chin and became very *grande dame*. "Mr. Dykes, really! This is absurd!"

"I haven't," said Dykes thoughtfully, "been called 'Mr.' in a dorg's age."

"Merely courtesy," Irene murmured.

Eliot giggled, and Bill said shortly, "For God's sake, let's get on with it."

Dykes looked at him. "I am not enjoying myself, Mr. Runson."

Bill closed his mouth tightly and dropped his eyes to his shoes. He'd better shut up. He was upset and he might say something silly. You couldn't live all those years in the same house with a person and not be jarred by her death. Mrs. Goodhue had been there before Irene left his father, and from then on. He'd never had much affection for her, certainly—she'd been too tart—but it had been a long time. He sighed and looked up at Dykes.

Irene had been telling her story and she ended with, "… and then I went to bed."

"Did you get out of bed again after you once got in?" Dykes asked.

Irene narrowed her eyes and said firmly, "No, I did not. I woke up with a headache at about six this morning, and I got up then and went to the bathroom for some aspirin."

"You found aspirin in the bathroom?"

"Yes."

"Did you see or hear anything while you were up?"

"Yes, I did."

"What?"

"I saw the bathroom, and the hall leading to the bathroom—it has really become a bit shabby, Bill—and I heard the water running when I turned on the faucet, and there were a couple of birds twirping outside."

Dykes said, "Thank you for the close attention to detail. Have you left anything out? Anything further you saw or heard?"

"No."

"Did you do anything else besides take aspirin?"

"No."

"Sure?"

"I am quite sure," said Irene. "Would you like to know what I was wearing when I took this trip?"

"Love to."

"I wore a nightgown of beige chiffon, deeply trimmed with a lace that has gold threads running through it, and a matching robe of gold cloth."

"How do you wash a costume like that?" Dykes asked.

"The nightgown washes very nicely. The robe has to be cleaned, of course."

Dykes nodded with his lips pursed, and Eliot giggled again. Madeleine said, "Will it be all right for me to get a footstool? If this is going to take long, I'd like to have a nap until I'm needed."

Dykes glanced at her and then at Eliot. "Will you provide a footstool for the young lady's feet?"

"Certainly." Eliot slid from his chair and was streaking for the hall when Dykes stopped him cold.

"Right in here, young man. There's one over there by the window."

"That one's merely for show," Eliot protested. "There's one in the hall—"

"Get the one by the window. If Mr. Runson objects, we can put a newspaper over it."

Eliot moved sulkily towards the window, and Bill observed, "It is pretty new, at that. I got it ten years ago, or thereabouts. Perhaps you'd better take your shoes off when you use it, Madeleine."

Madeleine calmly removed her shoes, and Irene threw her head back with a gay little laugh. "Bill, dear, you really *are* a doll."

Eliot retired to his chair, and Dykes said to him, "Mr. Runson, you are a cousin to this other Mr. Runson?"

"I have already said so."

"You have a salaried position in the concern that belongs to him. He's your boss. Don't you hate him?"

Eliot cast an easy half smile at Bill, and received a frown by way of return.

"Well, of course I hate him," Eliot said, enjoying himself. "Look at him, always frowning and cracking the whip. I very much fear that he hates me, too."

Madeleine wiggled her toes on the footstool. "I know how he feels. Here are some people who always make me want to frown."

Irene took it seriously. "But that isn't right. I believe you're suffering from some sort of complex, Bill. You should change your way of life, definitely."

Bill appeared to be studying his fingernails, and Madeleine spoke up for him again. "I expect Bill enjoys his own way of life quite well. You're forgetting that we all moved in on him without waiting for an invitation. Hasn't it occurred to either of you that he's bored to death with us?"

Eliot turned his highball glass in his hands and shrugged, and Irene dropped her eyes to the tapping toe of her slipper.

"You don't give a damn, either one of you," Madeleine went

on. "You're related to him, and he has money, so you camp on him for reasons of your own. If I were Bill, I'd shut the door in your faces. There are some people who don't want to spend all their time drinking, smoking, and saying smart things to each other."

"Madeleine, you are being impertinent!" Irene said furiously. "You know very well that I *never* impose on other people!"

"Well—" Eliot stretched his legs. "I'm the crown prince down at the business. Every time he gets a bit soft on a girl, I *have* to come in and protect my interests. If he marries and has children, where would *I* be?"

Irene laughed heartily. "Darling, you are *wonderful*."

Eliot nodded. "I've always thought so."

Dykes said, "None of you cared anything for Mrs. Goodhue."

Bill stood up and took a restless step or two. "She'd worked for me for a good many years. She wasn't what you'd call an affectionate type, but I was fond of her and I had respect for her. I don't understand how she could possibly have got caught inside that box."

"Oh, that's simple enough," Dykes said, watching him. "She had a bad wound on the head. Someone hit her and put her there."

Chapter Twelve

BILL SAT DOWN AGAIN ABRUPTLY, AND THERE WAS A HEAVY silence.

"Are you saying that Mrs. Goodhue was deliberately murdered?" Bill asked presently, in a stunned voice.

"What do *you* think?" Dykes said.

"But who would do such a thing, and why? How do you know she didn't injure her head getting into the box?"

"Why would she be getting into the box?"

Bill shook his head, and Eliot said quickly, "To catch up on the latest gossip."

Dykes was interested. "Do you mean that she was the type to go to such lengths to hear what people were saying?"

"Oh, definitely," Eliot said, his face brightening. "She always knew everything that went on. We all went downstairs to the dining room last night, you see, and—"

"I was merely interested in her habits," Dykes interrupted. "She didn't climb into the refrigerator to hear what was being said— the head wound was much too serious to have come from a bump. She was hit hard, her body pushed in there, and the door closed."

Irene said, "Oh, my God!"

Bill stood up again. "This—this is really bad. I'll do everything I can to help you. I'll have to tell you about the Reillys."

Dykes nodded with reserve, although his eyes had an eager glint, and Bill gave him the story of the two Reillys. He had just finished when a man appeared at the door, and Dykes turned around.

"What is it, Gus?"

"There's a dame downstairs who insists on cleaning up the place."

"Well—" Dykes shrugged. "The men are through, aren't they?" He turned to Bill. "Who is she?"

Bill shook his head.

"Name's Reilly," Gus supplied. "Says she's housekeeper here."

Dykes and Bill had disappeared before he'd finished speaking, and Gus's heavy eyebrows shifted upwards. "Where they going? To a fire?"

"You'd better follow them, fellow," Eliot said. "You might have to stand in front of Mrs. Reilly and draw your sword."

"Huh? Nuts," Gus said and departed, chewing gum.

Eliot looked at Irene and said quietly, "This is a mess."

She nodded. "I think we'll pack up and get out."

"I'm going to sneak up now and get my things," Eliot agreed. "You do the same, and we'll call a taxi and go together."

"Splendid!" Irene drew a long breath. "Come on, Madeleine. We'll have to pack in a hurry."

"No." Madeleine looked them over coldly. "We moved in on him without asking, and whatever you two do, I intend to ask him whether he wants me to go or whether I can help him by staying."

"Darling, you're so *difficult!*" Irene wailed. "If we wait that weird, beret creature may not let us go. Bill doesn't want us here. You *know* he doesn't. Heavens, I merely brought you here to try and make a match between you and Bill, but as things are, this is not the time, naturally."

"So you admit it."

"Yes, darling, I admit it. I'll admit anything. I'm at fault as usual, of course, and serves me right that it didn't work."

"What do you mean, it didn't work? I think he quite likes me."

Eliot stood up. "I'll slip along and get my things while you two make up your minds."

"Call the taxi," Irene said firmly. "We are *definitely* coming with you."

Eliot left the room and put in a call for a taxi and then flew upstairs. His bag was in Bill's room, and he flung his possessions into it and closed it. He thought regretfully of his pajamas and sheets, but decided that they'd have to wait for another time.

He returned to the library and found Madeleine there alone, looking sulky.

"Mother's packing," she said, glancing up at him. "She's packing for me, too, but I intend to wait until Bill comes back."

"You're being very silly," Eliot said sharply. "Bill can handle this thing perfectly well by himself, and it's going to be nasty around here."

"You go your way, and I'll go mine."

Eliot shrugged and departed for the front hall, where he heard Irene calling softly from upstairs.

"Eliot! Where are you? Help me with these bags."

Eliot put his own suitcase on the floor and ran up the stairs. He took two small bags from Irene and started down while she followed close behind.

"I packed only our most pressing things and left the rest. We can get them later. We have a couple of trunks in storage, and I can have those sent to us, just so that we get out of here now."

"Yes, of course."

They reached the front hall just as Bill and Dykes appeared from the back, and Bill gave them a long stare.

"Running? You're tired of my hospitality?"

"Bill, don't be unreasonable," Eliot protested. "It's Sunday night, and a weekend visit is always over on Sunday night."

Bill glanced at the clock. "It's only five, and I'd have expected you to ask me whether I need your help."

"Do you need my help?"

"No."

Dykes said, "Er—"

Irene cried, "Bill, dear, you *know* guests are only in the way when there's trouble."

Madeleine appeared and said, "Bill, Mother and Eliot seem to think we ought to go, but I'd like to know what you want us to do."

"May I have a word?" Dykes interposed.

Bill muttered, "What is it?"

"It would make things easier for me if they could stay over until tomorrow, at least. There will be new questions cropping up, and we could find out sooner who murdered Mrs. Goodhue."

"Oh, dear!" Irene said. "Do you *still* insist that she was murdered?"

"Certainly, madam, and you agree with me."

"What do you mean?" Irene demanded.

"You wouldn't be trying to dash off in such a hurry unless you were convinced that it was murder."

Irene gave him a glance of scorn which slid off him without leaving any mark, and Madeleine asked, "Did you get anything out of Mrs. Reilly?"

"Nothing much," Bill told her, "but we hope to get something from the son, Joe. He's on his way here now."

"Did you summon him?" Eliot asked.

"No. Mrs. Reilly told us he'd phoned to say he was on his way here, but she didn't care what he did, she was going to stay. As a matter of fact, she's cooking dinner for us now, which is something we all need. You and Irene, Eliot, more or less stuck your necks out when you first came here, so now you can stick it out until tomorrow and help Dykes all you can. It's murder, and it happened in my house, and I want it cleared up as soon as possible."

"Certainly, of course." Eliot settled his tie and cleared his throat. "But I live only a block away and I could at least sleep in my own place tonight. You can hardly suppose that I would relish sleeping up on that third floor." He paused to give a delicate shudder and then went on, "Nor do I relish the idea of sleeping with you again. After all, there won't be anyone around tonight to insure our rest by giving us dope."

Madeleine repeated, "Dope?" and Dykes turned his small blue eyes on Bill.

"You didn't tell me anything about being doped."

"Well, no." Bill gave his head a bothered shake. "There's been so much … We just assumed we'd been doped because someone cut off a piece of my hair last night without waking either one of us." He turned suddenly to Eliot. "If you were playing the clown and did it yourself, you'd better speak up. You know you mentioned that piece of hair several times, said I ought to paste it down."

Eliot denied it to high heaven and declared vociferously that he would never have closed an eye in a double bed with another person, had he not been given something to put him out.

"I wish you'd all sit down," Dykes said impatiently. "You haven't told me everything, and I must know things if I'm going to do this job properly. What *is* all this?"

Madeleine was the only one who sat down. Bill moved around restlessly while he tried to explain about his hair. He added that he and Eliot had tried to find out who had done the shearing, but had failed.

"You know, that *is* odd," Madeleine said from her chair. "Someone takes a lot of trouble to cut your front hair off, and Mrs. Reilly is obviously upset because you don't look so much like her son any more, and then someone else fills your bottle of hair oil with water so that that front piece will stick up and make you look as much like the son as possible."

Dykes looked at Bill again, and Bill felt his face flushing. He muttered, "I'd forgotten about the hair oil. I didn't think it meant anything, anyway."

"Sit down," Dykes said firmly, "until we find out what else has slipped all your minds."

"My dear man, *please!*" Irene almost stamped her foot. "I'm tired, I want a cocktail badly, and I must go and change, for I have a date tonight."

"You have no date, Mother," Madeleine said quietly. "I phoned and put it off when you were feeling so ill this morning."

"Darling, you really *should* mind your own business. Do you think it's going to improve my condition to stay here, with all that's going on?"

There was a knock on the front door, and they all jumped except Dykes, who went over and opened it. Joe Reilly stood outside, and he looked at Dykes in surprise, and then past him at Bill.

"Come in, Joe," Bill said. "I'm sorry about your mother, but she seems determined to stay here."

"Young man, did you ever see Mrs. Goodhue before your mother came to work here?" Dykes demanded.

"Oh, yes." Joe nodded. "She and Mother are old friends."

Chapter Thirteen

OUT OF AN UNCOMFORTABLE SILENCE, DYKES ASKED COLDLY, "Is this another thing that slipped all your minds?"

Bill began to be irritated. "Certainly not. I had no idea that they were friends. Matter of fact, I don't understand it—Mrs. Goodhue said nothing about Mrs. Reilly being an old friend of hers."

Mrs. Reilly's voice called from the back somewhere, "Dinner's ready, everybody. You must all come and eat it while it's nice and hot."

Joe frowned and shook his head. "She doesn't have to do this. I've told her so. She must come home with me."

"You can all go down and eat," Dykes said. "I want to question Mr. Joe Reilly, here."

Joe looked astounded, and Bill said, "Very well. Joe, there's been—"

"There's been a little trouble," Dykes interrupted smoothly. "I'd like to ask you a few questions. I'm, er, from the police."

Joe went pale and whispered, "What is it? Mother? She's—"

"She's all right," Dykes told him.

Bill urged the others towards the stairs and called back, "If you want something to eat later, Joe, come on down."

Joe and Dykes went off to the small back sitting room, and when the others reached the dining room, Eliot stopped suddenly and said in a voice of tragedy, "But we haven't had cocktails!"

"What are you talking about?" Bill said impatiently. "You've been drinking on and off all the afternoon."

"They were only bracers, and badly needed. I don't believe I can face my dinner without a cocktail or two."

Irene said, "Also."

Bill spoke through his closed teeth. "There'll be no cocktails served at this time. Those who can't eat will be good enough to sit quietly while those who can, do."

The three of them sat down quickly, but Bill paused with his hand on the back of his chair. "The days of the slavey are over. Mrs. Reilly cooked this meal, and there's no reason for her to limp in and out with the various dishes. Eliot, you and I will bring the food in."

Eliot arose with a little bow. "As you say, sir. *Noblesse oblige.*"

"*Noblesse* had better damn well *oblige* in a hurry," Bill said and made for the kitchen, with Eliot trotting along behind.

Irene gave a silvery little laugh, and Madeleine murmured, "Feeling better, Mother?"

"I am feeling simply frightful," Irene declared, "but I hope I still have a sense of humor. Eliot really is a love. Don't you find him amusing?"

"Yes," said Madeleine, "he's a scream."

"Why don't you scream, then?"

"I don't dare. I wouldn't be able to stop."

The two men returned with bowls of food which they placed in the middle of the table. Each bowl had a spoon sticking up in it, and Eliot explained, "You see, we pass the bowls around, and each person is supposed to take some out and put it on his plate. Don't attempt to eat from the bowl, and don't take more than your share."

"Thanks on behalf of Madeleine and myself," Bill said. "Apparently you and Irene won't be eating, anyway."

Irene smiled wanly. "We are going to *try*, for your sake."

Eliot nodded. "If this unrecognizable food is what the house provides, without the buffer of a cocktail, we shall munch on it as courteously as possible."

"Seems to be your only course," Bill agreed equably. "Munch or go hungry."

"If you'll excuse me for being dull and serious for a moment," Madeleine said, "how is it that Mrs. Reilly can go ahead and cook, like this, if Mrs. Goodhue was her dear friend? What did she say when she found out about it?"

"We didn't tell her that Mrs. Goodhue had been murdered," Bill explained. "We said she'd been taken ill and died suddenly, and Mrs. Reilly clicked her tongue and passed the remark that she'd always told her not to sleep with her windows open at night."

"Didn't she want to know what had caused her death?" Eliot asked.

"No. She told *us*. Said it was pneumonia."

Irene, pushing the food about on her plate with her fork, shook her head a little. "Those people usually save their solicitude for the funeral."

"She wanted to see the body to pay her respects," Bill went on. "When we told her that it had been taken away, she smiled at me and said that she just knew I'd give Mrs. Goodhue the best possible funeral. Said she'd gladly attend and thought she'd buy a new dress for the occasion."

"What *was* Mrs. Goodhue like?" Madeleine asked wonderingly. "Nobody seems to care much about her death."

"I care," Bill said soberly. "She—had a lot of good points."

Eliot looked up from his plate. "Name one."

"Oh, Eliot!" Irene dropped her fork. "*Everybody* has *some* good points. It's not nice to speak ill of the dead."

Bill shook his head and changed the subject abruptly. "Madeleine, I didn't know that you were a professional pianist. Where do you play?"

"Oh, she was just boasting," Irene said quickly. "She had one engagement. It wasn't nice. She—"

"Mother, why don't you admit that your day is done? I know there are still plenty of girls who earn their living by getting married, but it isn't necessary today, not if you don't like that type of job. I think it's perfectly absurd that I have to keep my professional career a secret."

Irene moaned, "Oh, my God! Be quiet, will you?"

Bill glanced from one to the other of them. "Why does she have to keep it a secret, Irene? Surely playing the piano is no disgrace."

"No," Irene agreed bitterly, "not if she played in concerts. But what she does *is* simply *disgraceful!*"

"Oh, do you mean last night?" Bill asked. "And Inavsy? What does he do?"

"He *whistles*," Irene whispered tragically. "And *my* daughter, dressed in come-hither clothes, accompanies him on the piano."

Eliot started to laugh and couldn't seem to stop, but Madeleine frowned. "They're not come-hither clothes. They're merely theatrical, and anyway, Inavsy whistles very well. I have a good chance of getting into the big time, and I don't mean dull concerts where the meager audience creep in and sit coughing and blowing their noses."

Irene's voice became shrill. "Darling, Inavsy is *cheap*. You know he is."

"He's a hard worker, Mother, and I'm having my chance to appear in New York. I might get somewhere. My contract expires when he returns to Paris."

"Sounds fair enough," Bill said. "He's a stepping stone for her. Anyway, I admire her for doing something."

"You stay out of this, you old stick-in-the-mud." But Irene's voice had returned to its natural pitch.

Eliot's laughter rose again, and Bill said fiercely, "Shut up! Irene, I may be a stick-in-the-mud, but you're an old-fashioned stuffed shirt."

Irene shrieked, "What?"

"Yes, you are. You have interesting groups of friends and you enjoy your life, but nobody, to your way of thinking, is anybody or anything unless they live just your way, which makes you a narrow, bigoted—well—stuffed shirt."

"You're under a strain, Bill," Irene said carefully, "and so I make allowances for you. As a matter of fact, no one could be more alien to my way of life than you, and yet I brought my only daughter here to try and make a match between you."

"I would not have considered your daughter unless she'd made her mark at something," Bill replied. "And I don't mean debutante."

"Ah, well," Madeleine sighed, "that gives me a glimmer of hope, anyway."

Bill laughed, and Eliot and Irene exchanged glances.

"He always did laugh at the wrong places," Eliot said.

Irene raised her eyebrows. "What do you find amusing, Bill?"

"The whole silly conversation."

"Then I'm oversensitive, perhaps. You have just insulted my daughter."

"I have not insulted your daughter. I was making a point."

"You insulted me, all right," Madeleine said cheerfully. "You said you wouldn't even consider me until I proved myself worthy of you. The insinuation was that you could never love me for myself alone."

Bill turned to her and put his elbow on the table. "You're deliberately twisting my words around. You know perfectly well what I mean, and you agree with me. Anybody who thinks only of the next date is an uninteresting vegetable." He paused for a glimpse at Irene and Eliot and added hastily, "Not to everybody, of course, but to me, and I think you're the same. There are other things in life besides just boy and girl."

"Not for a woman," Irene said decidedly.

Madeleine turned on her. "Bill's right. You *are* a stuffed shirt when you make a statement like that. It's all right for you to go out on date after date and enjoy it, but it's not for me. I liked only the first year of it. There's nothing more boring to me now— night after night—drinking, eating, dancing—talk, talk, talk— all about boy and girl. When I go out to play accompaniment to that lousy whistler, I find it more entertaining."

Irene devoted herself to a thumbnail and said silkily, "All right, darling. I am wrong, of course, and you are right. You must lead your own life and do as you think best."

"Thanks. And for heaven's sake, let this be the last time you try to push me into marriage."

"Yes, dear. I don't seem to have been very subtle about it, do I?"

"No."

"No harm done," Bill said comfortably. "As far as I'm concerned, I'm very much attracted, and perhaps in the course of time, Madeleine will be attracted to me."

"How on earth did you think that up?" Eliot asked admiringly.

"It's away above your usual standard of blundering."

Irene stood up. "I suppose dinner is over? Eliot, do give me your arm. I really need change and rest at this point."

They departed, and Bill turned to Madeleine, who was still sitting at the table.

She looked up at him. "You know, she *wasn't* very subtle about it, was she?"

Chapter Fourteen

BILL DROPPED BACK INTO HIS CHAIR AND GAVE MADELEINE A questioning look.

"It isn't like Mother to be so obvious. The other prospects she's had for me—well, I didn't realize it until afterwards, and they never realized it."

"What do you mean, exactly?"

"Oh, I don't know, except that it occurred to me she might have come here for some other reason than that of making a match between us."

Bill was silent for a moment while he thought it over, and then he said slowly, "You know, she said she was desperate. Something interrupted at the time, and I just put it down to her worry over you—your unmarried state."

Madeleine shook her head a little. "Desperate? She's very annoyed with me and she won't let me live alone. I must live with her. I'm only twenty-two, and my profession is a dark secret, and I must dress quite differently for my social and my professional life so that no one will recognize me. But—desperate! Of course, Mother has an exaggerated way of speaking, and perhaps this is just a shift in tactics. I always lost my temper when I found out about her maneuvers to get me married, so perhaps she figures it might work if she brings everything out into the open."

"I suppose that's all it is." Bill stood up. "Let's go."

"Wait a minute." She pushed back her chair. "As you say, the service needs a little help, these days. I'll carry these dishes out to Mrs. Reilly."

Bill helped her, and they found Mrs. Reilly sitting at the kitchen table eating her own dinner. She smiled up at him and said, "That's real nice of you. I never had such a good employer."

"But your son told me you had never done this sort of work before."

Mrs. Reilly laughed and shook her head. "Joe, now, he's sort of old-fashioned. I've had these jobs before. You get the most, this way, and I've been able to give my boys a good education. See, Joe wants me to live with him, but I know better. Joe should get married and live his own life, and I wouldn't want to live with them. I always say there's no house big enough for two families."

"Well, but Joe isn't married," Bill said.

"No, sir, but if he lived alone he might get married. I've been living with him for several years, and Joe don't do much but come home and maybe take me to a movie. I know he should be going out with a girl, so when this job came along, I just up and took it."

"How did this job come along?" Bill asked. "Did you see the ad in the paper?"

"No, sir. Mrs. Goodhue told me about it."

"Oh? When was that?"

"Why, the day b, but then I got cold feet. But I came back the next day. And now that Mrs. Goodhue is dead, you'll need me, so I'm going to stay."

Bill looked at her for a moment and then asked, "Why would Mrs. Goodhue tell you about this job when she needed it herself?"

"Oh, well. She was going to leave sometime, and she told me I could get it."

"Were you surprised to see me looking so much like your son?"

Mrs. Reilly shook her head vaguely. "Why, no. Mrs. Goodhue told me, but she said for me not to say anything about it."

"Why not?"

Mrs. Reilly fingered the handle of her coffee cup absently. "Well, I don't rightly know. She was finding out something for me. I'll tell you sometime, not now. I don't know …"

Her voice trailed off, and when he tried to prod her further, she became suddenly brisk.

"I'm busy right now. I'll tell you some other time."

"Now's the time."

"No, it isn't."

He said flatly, "Do you realize that Mrs. Goodhue was murdered?"

"Don't be silly. She got pneumonia, as I knew and told her she would."

"No," Bill said, watching her. "Someone locked her up in the refrigerator."

Mrs. Reilly laughed. "With all the butter and eggs and things? Such nonsense."

"I mean the old box," Bill said, swinging the door open. "You see, it's empty."

Mrs. Reilly walked over and peered in. She was silent for a moment, and then she said, "Well! You mean she got locked up in here?"

Bill nodded soberly. "Someone put her here—killed her. You should tell me anything that you know about her so that we can find out who did it."

Mrs. Reilly shook her head several times. "But I'm not exactly surprised. She was a mean one, upon my soul. I guess somebody got even with her."

"Yes. Now, tell me who wanted to get even with her."

"How should I know?"

"Perhaps you don't," Bill said quietly, "but you'll tell me what Mrs. Goodhue was trying to find out for you, and what you were going to reveal to me someday, or you will leave here immediately."

Mrs. Reilly looked up at him, and her eyes filmed with tears. She whispered, "Oh, no!"

"Tell me."

She sat down and wiped her eyes with a corner of her apron. After a short silence she said painfully, "Mrs. Goodhue told me you looked like my poor dead son and that she wanted me to work here occasionally when she took a trip, even though I'd given up this kind of work, due to Joe. She said it would make me feel much better, being with you. See, I was grieving a lot about my boy. She said it would be like he was alive again. She didn't want anyone else coming into the house who maybe wouldn't get out after she came back from her trip."

"She didn't say anything to me about a trip. I suppose she was going to visit her native Scotland?"

"Yes." Mrs. Reilly sighed. "She was going to find out if my son had a proper funeral."

"Where did he die?"

"In Scotland."

"What was he doing there?"

Mrs. Reilly pleated her apron over her knees with nervous fingers. "He—went back to look up a girl. See, he was there during the war and he met this girl, and he went back. But he got killed in an accident, and I couldn't rest, worrying whether he got a decent funeral, so Mrs. Goodhue was going to find out, to ease my mind."

Bill considered it and then said, "All right," rather abruptly and left the kitchen. He noticed that the dining-room table had been cleared, and at the same moment, Madeleine loomed up at his elbow.

"It's all right. I fully expected to have to do it single-handed. And I, personally, do not believe one word of Mrs. Reilly's story. She made it up as she went along."

"Why do you say that? It sounded all right to me."

"Nope. Something wrong with it."

They went upstairs together and came upon Irene and Eliot standing with their ears glued to the door of the little back sitting room. Bill frowned at them, and they moved off together with quiet grace.

Madeleine suppressed a giggle and then followed Bill on tiptoe as he went and put his own ear against the door.

Dykes's voice came to them quite clearly. "But, young man, you've already said that you were in agreement that your mother could come here and work, so how can I accept the fact that you suddenly changed your mind without a reason?"

Joe sounded very tired. "I didn't know. I couldn't know that he looked so much like my brother."

"Why should that make a difference?"

"She ought to forget my brother. It isn't good for her to be staying here just because of the resemblance. Can't you see that? It brings up memories. It's morbid."

"Doesn't seem to have worked that way," Dykes said. "She's happy here. There's something more to it than that."

"There isn't—there is not! That's all there is to it."

"Well ... I still think you cut off Mr. Runson's hair."

Joe's voice rose to a scream. "I did not!"

"All right. No need to yell. But I still don't know why Mrs. Goodhue sent your mother here."

"I've told you. She wanted someone she knew to hold down the job for her while she took a trip to her birthplace in Scotland."

"That's where your brother died, in an accident."

"Yes—yes—I've told you."

"So Mrs. Goodhue must have put water in Mr. Runson's hair lotion to make his hair stick up in front so that he'd look more like your brother."

"What? Water? Mrs. Goodhue?"

"It must have been Mrs. Goodhue. She seems to have gone to a lot of trouble."

Joe said, "I've told you all I know. I'm tired."

"You haven't told me why you're so desperate to get your mother away from here."

"Can't you understand a man's wanting his mother to stop working when he has enough to support her? It makes me ashamed. She's worked all her life. She sent me to college, and it wasn't easy."

"Why did you say she had never done this type of work before?"

"I've told you a thousand times," Joe said, his voice cracking a little. "I'll admit it's false pride, but I'm educated and I don't want it known that she worked as a servant all her life."

"Yeah, sure. But you agreed to let her come here and take Mrs. Goodhue's place. So, why?"

"I've told you that, too. She begged and pleaded—said it would be for only a short time, and I could tell our friends she was off on a trip. She argued that she'd be able to buy a couple of things we wanted, a car and a television set. I couldn't hold out. I should have. I was selfish and I bitterly regret it, now."

"O.K.," Dykes said, "I'll take your word for it. I'd prefer that you and your mother stay here tonight, though."

Joe cried, "No! No—I must get to the office tomorrow. I can't go from here, it's too far. We'll have to leave now. You have our address. I'll get Mother."

"Your mother's not going with you. She told us she didn't care what you said or did this time, she was staying right here."

There was no answer from Joe, but after a moment they heard a dull thud, and they knew that he had fainted again.

Chapter Fifteen

MADELEINE AND BILL PUSHED INTO THE LITTLE SITTING ROOM and bumped into Dykes, who was hurrying out to get help. He clutched at his beret and glared at them.

"How long have you been listening outside?"

"Later," Bill said briefly. "Madeleine, go down and get Mrs. Reilly."

Madeleine nodded and went off, and Bill made for the phone.

"What are you doing?" Dykes demanded.

"I'm getting a doctor. This is the second time he's fainted in this house, and I think someone should look at him."

The doctor was a college friend of Bill's who had just set up in private practice, and he promised to come at once, with, Bill thought, more eagerness than dignity.

Dykes was kneeling on the floor slapping at one of Joe's wrists, and he asked over his shoulder, "When was the other time he fainted here?"

Bill came over and began to slap the other wrist. "I'm sure I told you. When he first came here, last night. He took one look at me, and presumably I was so like his brother that it knocked him cold."

Madeleine came in carrying a cup of tea, and was followed by Mrs. Reilly, who appeared to be quite calm. She sat down on a chair near Joe and reached over to stroke his forehead. He was beginning to stir, and she said, "Joe … come on, Joe."

Dykes cleared his throat. "Mrs. Reilly, you know this boy is delicate. Why didn't you tell him that Mr. Runson looks so much like your other son?"

"I didn't know he'd get to see him," Mrs. Reilly answered simply. "I had to get him to bring my things over, but I thought I'd be answering the door, or Mrs. Goodhue."

"You knew she was coming back?"

"Oh, yes. She told me when to come here, a month ago. She said she'd come back to show me the ropes for a few days before she left again. See?"

Joe tried to get up, and Bill and Dykes helped him into a chair. Mrs. Reilly moved over beside him and started to feed him the tea, and Dykes urged Bill out into the hall.

"That was interesting, huh?"

"Was it?" said Bill. "And here I thought I was being bored."

"Mind if I look around your bedroom?"

"No, but why?"

"You come with me," Dykes said.

Bill followed him up the stairs, and when they got to his bedroom, he noticed that Madeleine was with them. She was being very quiet and unobtrusive, and Dykes did not seem to notice when she moved over and stood against the wall.

"Which side of the bed do you sleep on?"

Bill glanced at the tossed covers and dented pillows and gestured. "On the farther side, there." He added, "Er, what with the confusion, today, these rooms haven't been tidied."

Dykes nodded. "I was banking on that." He examined the bed and then got down on his hands and knees and crawled around the end and towards the door. When he got there, he stood up and seemed to lose himself in thought for a moment before he turned to a small table with a lamp on it which stood close to the door. He examined it closely, starting at the top and working slowly down to the bottom and onto the floor, where he suddenly and triumphantly picked up something.

Madeleine and Bill had been watching in silence, but when Dykes pulled out a handkerchief and made wrapping motions with it, they were unable to see anything at all.

"What is it?" Bill asked. "You didn't find anything."

"Oh, yes I did. In fact, I found what I was looking for." He returned the handkerchief to his pocket with an air of confidence and settled his beret.

"Now, I'd like to see Mrs.—hmm—Mrs. Wisner's room."

"Certainly not," Madeleine said sharply.

Dykes was a bit startled and he swung around on her quickly. "Oh, Miss Smith. I didn't know you were here. Perhaps you could take me to your mother's room."

"Why?"

"It's necessary for me to check up on something. Mr. Runson, I'm trying to investigate a murder."

"Yes." Bill looked over at Madeleine. "It doesn't matter, surely? We mustn't do anything to hinder this thing. Dykes has a job to do, and if he wants to go in there …"

"Don't you think we should ask Mother first?"

"No, no," Dykes said hastily. "It won't take a minute."

"I expect your mother's enjoying a cocktail with Eliot and wouldn't want to be disturbed," Bill suggested.

"Nom a highball," Madeleine said absently. She shrugged. "I'll go with you, but I can't see what you expect to find in Mother's bedroom. She couldn't have had anything to do with all this."

Bill thought she looked frightened, and was reminded of her perplexity at Irene's lack of subtlety in trying to match her up with himself.

Irene's room was as untidy as Bill's had been. The bed was unmade and the dressing table was littered with boxes and bottles and covered with a fine spray of powder.

"Mother's used to living in hotels," Madeleine said. "It hasn't occurred to her that there's no service today."

Dykes went straight to the closet and opened the door. He searched briefly, and then came out and began to go slowly over the carpet. He started at the dressing table and made his way over to the door and then back to the dressing table, where he went down on his hands and knees. Once again he picked up what appeared to be nothing and carefully folded it into the same handkerchief.

"He needs a vacation," Madeleine whispered. "His head's ailing."

But Dykes seemed to be in high good humor. "Has the garbage

gone out today?" he asked politely.

Bill raised his shoulders. "I doubt it, since it's Sunday."

"Ah, yes, of course. I'll go down."

Bill followed, and Madeleine trailed them. She muttered out of the corner of her mouth to Bill, "He *is* demented."

"No, he's looking for my piece of hair. I told him it was in the garbage."

"The hair!"

Dykes went straight to the kitchen and opened the lid of the garbage pail. It was filled to the top, and he straightened up and looked around at Madeleine and Bill.

They stood where they were, just inside the kitchen door. Their faces wore identical expressions, a combination of fear that Dykes might ask them to help him sift through the garbage and stolid determination to refuse any such request.

Dykes interpreted their reactions correctly and gave up the idea of asking for their cooperation. He walked to the door that opened onto an areaway which had steps leading to the front sidewalk and called shortly, "Hank!"

Hank appeared at once. His tall, thin frame was clad in plain clothes, and he appeared to be some days away from a good grooming. He chewed gum in much the same manner that he breathed.

Dykes said, "Get some newspaper and shovel this garbage out bit by bit. I'm looking for something."

Hank's expression and the movement of his jaws underwent no change. He glanced around the kitchen, his eyes passing over Madeleine and Bill without curiosity, and at last spotted a pile of newspapers on the undershelf of a small table. He went over and picked out a few, and then used a spoon which was lying in the sink for a shovel. He lifted out the garbage piece by piece and paused over each spoonful until Dykes told him to go on.

Mrs. Reilly came into the kitchen and stopped in her tracks, staring.

"What are they doing?"

"Looking for something," Bill said. "How's Joe?"

"He's all right, now. He wants to go home, but he won't go

without me. Only I'm not going."

"Well, tell him I'll come and help him to the room he had last night."

"Yes, but he's got to go to work in the morning, and it's too far from here."

Bill gave it up, and Mrs. Reilly went into her bedroom. She emerged again almost immediately and stood looking at Dykes and Hank. They had just finished, and Dykes seemed distinctly annoyed. "Put it back," he said shortly.

"Whatever were you looking for?" Mrs. Reilly asked.

Dykes glanced at her. "Perhaps you've seen it. I want that piece of hair that was cut off Mr. Runson's head. Did you see it in the garbage?"

Mrs. Reilly looked down and carefully smoothed her apron, and Dykes stopped frowning and became alert.

"Oh. What did you do with it?"

"Well, I saw it lying there, and I thought maybe I ought to save it. I washed it off. See, I thought Mr. Runson might want to give it to someone, or put it away for when he's older."

Hank's dead pan showed the first sign of cracking, but managed to stand the strain, and Madeleine said, "That was thoughtful of you. He can have a watch fob made of it." She added almost immediately, "What *is* a watch fob?"

"May I see it, please?" Dykes said to Mrs. Reilly. "I'll give it back to you."

"You will?" She seemed pleased, and limped off quite cheerfully to her bedroom. She returned with the curl, and Dykes pulled out his carefully wrapped handkerchief and opened it on the table. Bill and Madeleine moved closer and saw that the handkerchief contained a few wisps of hair, too few to have been visible from any distance.

Dykes pulled a wisp from the curl, and matched it with the other. It seemed to fit, and he straightened up with a satisfied grunt. He returned the curl to Mrs. Reilly, said, "Thank you," and gave a completely unintelligible command to Hank, who promptly returned from whence he came. Dykes left by another door, and it seemed that the show was over for the time being.

Bill turned to Mrs. Reilly. "Since you saved the curl for me, you might as well give it to me. Maybe I can have a switch made out of it."

She closed her hand quickly and said, "No—oh, no. I—I found it. I'll keep it."

She disappeared into her room, and Bill turned away. Madeleine was laughing, but she composed her face and said, "I don't know what that Dykes is getting at. He found the wisp of hair in your room, which seems natural enough, and I saw what he picked up in Mother's room. He didn't open the handkerchief out, but I saw it glittering through, and I know what it was—a piece of her gold dressing robe. It shreds, and it's only to be expected that there'd be a scrap lying on her carpet, so what's it all about?"

Bill looked at her for a silent moment and then sighed. "Think it over, and face it. His subsequent actions and all that. Don't you realize that he found the piece of gold in *my* room—and the wisp of hair in *Irene's* room?"

Chapter Sixteen

MADELEINE'S FACE WAS PALE, AND SHE SAID IN A LOW VOICE, "Oh, no!"

Bill took her arm. "Let's go up. He's probably talking to her now."

They found Irene in the library, sitting with Dykes and Eliot in a cozy group. Dykes gave them only a brief glance, and they sat down quietly. Eliot, who had slid fluidly to his feet at Madeleine's entrance, dropped back into his chair again.

Dykes was saying, "So you see it *is* odd that someone should snip off your host's front hair."

Eliot said, "Mm."

Irene laughed. "*I* think somebody did it because he simply couldn't stand the sight of it sticking up like that."

Dykes gave a false laugh and then composed his face again. "You know, I think I agree with you. I believe it was done because someone thought it spoiled his looks. In fact, *you* thought it spoiled his looks, so you must have done it, Mrs. Wisner."

Irene lost color behind her makeup and gave a little scream. "*I?* Absurd!"

"You," Dykes said gravely. "I have clues which make me quite sure of it. You went in during the night, turned on the lamp on that little table near the door, went around the bed, cut off the hair, and left the room after turning off the lamp again. You returned to your own room and found that you were still holding the piece of hair. You decided that you'd better put it well away from you, so you went downstairs and dropped it into the garbage pail."

Irene raised her highball glass to her lips and drank with her eyes lowered.

"You might as well admit it because I know you did it."

Irene replaced her glass, raised her eyes, and gave Dykes a mischievous little smile. "Oh, well. Daddy used to spank me for pranks like this, but you can only scold me. I really couldn't stand that cockatoo any more. He looks *much* better without it."

Dykes cast a rather bleak look at Bill. "I never saw him with it so I wouldn't know."

"His beauty is highly debatable, anyway," Eliot said on a sighing breath.

Irene laughed, but there was an uneasy note in the sound. "Darling, *don't* be jealous. He has nothing approaching your style, of course, but his features are not bad at all."

"You seem to have gone to a lot of trouble to improve his looks," Dykes observed, "putting a drug in his coffee."

"Oh, pooh, just a couple of my sleeping pills. I dropped them in the coffeepot. They don't do much for me, but the others seem to have slept like hogs. I slept fairly well, as a matter of fact, but I *did* wake up and cut off that silly curl, just as you said. I think it's rather marvelous of you to have found out. You might have been there, the way you describe it."

Dykes was unimpressed by this flattery and merely said, "You planned the thing in advance."

Irene looked down at her fingernails. "Oh, nonsense! It was a silly whim. I keep the pills in my purse because it's necessary to take them some little time before I go to bed."

"Pretty strong drug."

"Perhaps they are, but my doctor prescribes them for me, and I need them."

"Yes. Well, now tell me why you cut off the piece of hair."

"But—" She made a helpless little gesture with her hands. "We've just been *over* all that. I wanted to make him more handsome."

"No." Dykes shook his head. "Not just that. You wouldn't have gone to so much trouble for a prank. You'd better tell me."

Irene looked full at him, and her smile was winsome, with a

touch of pathos. "This is very embarrassing, and my daughter will be simply furious. I'm a born matchmaker and I was trying to promote a marriage between her and Bill. But how *could* she fall in love with him with that stupid curl waving in the breeze at the top of his head? So I cut it off, that's all." She stood up. "You'll have to excuse me. I've had a headache all day."

Dykes rose and said politely, "I'm sorry about your headache, but if you would answer a few more questions before you go, I would appreciate it."

She paused, but her face was mutinous.

"When you took that piece of hair down to the garbage pail, were there any lights on downstairs?"

Irene looked thoughtful and said slowly, "Yes. Now that you mention it, I believe there were. The kitchen was lighted."

"How about the hall leading to the kitchen, from the bottom of the stairs?"

"Yes. Yes, I believe so. I didn't have to fumble along in the dark, you see. Now, I really must go. Good night."

Dykes bowed her out and came back to survey the others. Eliot was pulling at his lip, and Madeleine watched her hands as they moved restlessly in her lap. Bill raised his head with a questioning look on his face.

Dykes knew that they had no intention of commenting, so he settled his beret and observed, "I suppose, Mr. Runson, that that curl on your head was entirely too much for a fastidious person like Mrs. Wisner."

Madeleine looked up eagerly. "That's right. Mother can get really fussed about trivial things sometimes. She'll go to ridiculous lengths."

Eliot gave a laugh that sounded foolish even to his own ears. "Oh, yes. She's straightened my tie several times. She likes things to be right."

Bill nodded. "I remember she used to move the furniture around a lot in order to get it as she thought it should be."

Dykes distributed an odd smile among them. "I'll be going, now. I expect to return in the morning. Thanks for your cooperation. If that young fellow, Joe, goes home tonight, please get his address for me. I don't want to disturb him or his mother any further."

Bill assured him most earnestly that Joe's address would be treated as the crown jewels, and the three of them ushered him out the front door.

Madeleine went upstairs to join her mother immediately, and Eliot delicately wiped his brow.

"Such a pleasure to be rid of him, even if it's only for tonight."

Bill sighed. "I suppose we'd better give Joe an arm up to his bedroom, or put him in a taxi. I wonder whether Mrs. Reilly will be afraid to sleep downstairs tonight?"

Eliot echoed the sigh. "Let's get going. I know I'd be afraid to sleep anywhere in this house tonight."

"Suits me. I don't want you in my bed. Come on."

They went back to the little sitting room, where they found Mrs. Reilly dozing in a chair. Joe was lying on a couch, his eyes wide open, staring at nothing.

He looked at them as they came in, and Bill said, "Would you like to sleep here tonight, Joe, or do you feel well enough to go home? I'll get you a taxi."

"It's as you please," Joe replied indifferently. "I can't go to the office tomorrow, anyway. I never can work the next day after one of these attacks. I'll have to phone them."

Eliot nodded seriously. "I shan't be able to go in in the morning, either."

"Oh, yes, you shall," Bill said grimly. "You and I will both be there, on time. You know we're badly behind."

Eliot said something under his breath, and Bill turned to Joe. "We'll take you upstairs. Would you like anything to eat before you go?"

Joe nodded. "I'll go downstairs for it, myself. I prefer to sit at a table when I eat. Mother will get me something. Mother!"

Mrs. Reilly woke up and asked composedly, "Yes? What is it?"

Bill and Eliot went down to the kitchen with them. Bill had suggested that Eliot leave, but Eliot sighed, "No, I'll have to wait and help you get him upstairs."

"I'd suppose that you were being unusually thoughtful," Bill said, "if I didn't know that you intend to sit in on whatever Mrs. Reilly dishes up."

"Erase the superiority," Eliot remarked briefly. "So do you."

Mrs. Reilly was delighted to have Bill sit down to a bite with Joe, but she obviously considered Eliot just a nuisance. Joe gave them each a glance of disfavor, but said nothing.

Bill asked Mrs. Reilly if she'd like to change to a room upstairs that was near someone, but she shook her head and said comfortably, "No, no. I'm not afraid. I like it here. That fella, now, he's just trying to make himself sound important. I don't think she ever was shut up in that box. She was a sneaky one, you know, always up to something. It serves her right."

Joe said, "Mother! Please!"

She ignored him and put some cold meat on the table, and some bread and butter. She added three glasses of milk and then put her hand on Bill's shoulder and lowered her head to his.

"I'm tired. I guess I'll go to bed. See that they put the food away when they've finished."

She retired to her room, and Bill and Joe began to eat. Eliot sat looking at the glass of milk in front of him.

"Try it," Bill suggested. "It's quite highly regarded in some quarters."

Eliot sipped and said, "Eek!" He helped himself to meat and bread and butter, and began to butter his slice of bread, which he held in the palm of one hand, with the large kitchen knife which Mrs. Reilly had put beside his plate.

Joe looked up and said, "I don't think that's very funny."

"Nor do I," Eliot agreed. "More along the lines of tragedy, especially if I slice off a thumb."

"Mother knows perfectly well how to serve, but this job isn't serious to her. She cuts corners when she's tired."

"There's no criticism intended," Bill soothed him. "It was nice of her to get us anything at all. But Joe, you know we heard something of Dykes's questioning of you tonight. He hadn't finished with you when you passed out on him, and he'll be back tomorrow. If you're not here, he'll follow you, and I'd advise you to tell

him what you know. It's the quickest way out for you. After that"—
Bill lowered his voice—"I'll send your mother back to you."

Joe rubbed a tired hand across his forehead. "I know, I've been
thinking there are a few extra things I should tell him. I hate to,
but I suppose I must—be better in the end."

"It will be better," Bill agreed, "because he'll find out, anyway."

"Yes. I knew Mrs. Goodhue had some sort of plan. She'd been
dropping in frequently during the past month. And Mother had
blossomed out—seemed happier. Of course I didn't know what it
was, and they wouldn't talk while I was there. I knew Mother
wasn't being sent up here just so that Mrs. Goodhue could make
a trip, and I didn't know, and still don't know, how your resemblance to my brother ties in." He made the same weary gesture
with his hand across his forehead. "I'll have to tell him, though,
that when I objected to Mother's working again, Mrs. Goodhue
took me aside and told me that it was necessary for Mother to
come here, as something had to be done which would benefit us
all."

Chapter Seventeen

BILL AND ELIOT BOTH EXCLAIMED, BUT JOE MERELY LOOKED gloomily at his plate.

"That means that there was some definite plan," Eliot said tensely. "Probably blackmail. You must know what it was, Joe."

"I know nothing about it," Joe declared peevishly. "I've thought and thought, but I can't even guess. I've tried to question Mother and she won't answer me. Mrs. Goodhue must have put the pressure on her to keep quiet about it, and yet it was Mrs. Goodhue who took me aside and told me we'd be benefited."

"Money?" Bill said wonderingly.

"She wouldn't say anything more, although I tried to question her. When you've never had money, you're sometimes tempted to do things against your conscience, so I kept quiet until Mother phoned me to bring her suitcase here. It was all packed and ready. You can imagine the shock I got when I saw you."

"Do I actually look all that much like your brother?"

"It was that black curl," Joe said, sighing. "He had a black curl that stuck up in just the same way. You can see how I feel. I knew something was going on, and now that woman's been murdered. I don't understand it. I don't know anything, but I *must* get Mother home."

He was pale and sweating, and Bill said hastily, "Look here, you mustn't worry about it just now. Try and eat something, and I'll send her back to you, I promise."

Joe finished his milk, but seemed unable to eat very much. They helped him up to the room he'd occupied the night before and found the bed neatly made and Eliot's pajamas folded on top.

96

Joe explained that he'd made the bed himself. "I've always done that and tidied my room so that Mother wouldn't have so much to do."

They left him and were heading for the stairs when Bill stopped. "Let's look around in Mrs. Goodhue's room. We might find something that Dykes overlooked. After all, he didn't know that she intended to make money out of my resemblance to Mrs. Reilly's son."

Eliot turned around in silence, and they went back to Mrs. Goodhue's room. They were conscious of Joe's presence next door, and went in quietly and without speaking.

The room was exquisitely neat, and they spent only a brief time among the orderly arrangement of her clothes. They moved over to the desk, where it was apparent that she had not been a magpie type. There was writing paper, pen, and ink, and a few letters which they read, and which were mostly from a relative in Scotland. They glanced hastily through a photograph album, and then Eliot picked up a telephone directory. "What did she want with this, up here?" he asked in a low voice.

Bill shook his head. "Maybe she kept it to look up addresses."

"Hmm. Here's an address written in pencil on the cover."

Bill glanced down at it. "Doesn't say what it's the address of."

"Of what the address—no, of whom does the address belong, or—"

"Shut up," said Bill. "There's always an address written on the front of any telephone book."

There seemed to be nothing more there, and they presently went down to Bill's room, where Eliot glanced around to make sure that he'd left none of his possessions. Bill was tired and anxious to be rid of him, and he practically ran him down to the front hall.

Madeleine was there, her eyes looking big and dark in her pale face.

"Mother's ill. I think I'll have to get a doctor. She can't sleep, she has a violent headache and she's nauseated."

Bill went with her to the phone, and Eliot gave his suitcase a little kick and then headed towards the library.

"Don't touch the liquor," Bill called after him.

"What do you mean?" Eliot demanded. "How can I drink it without touching it?"

"You've had enough. I want you in the office bright and early in the morning."

Eliot returned slowly, muttering, "Life with you would be utterly grim and boring."

"You're hurting my feelings," Bill said. "I thought you'd become quite fond of me."

"I loathe every bone in your body."

"Why don't you go home?"

"How can I go home? Irene so ill. What's wrong with *her* anyway?"

"How should I know?"

"You shouldn't." Eliot kicked his suitcase again. "It makes me nervous. Is it coincidence, or poison?"

"Poison!"

Eliot said, "Be quiet!" as Madeleine approached.

"He's sending someone over right away," she told them.

"Isn't he coming himself?" Bill asked.

"Oh, no. He never goes out at night, any more. He sends a younger man."

"Why? Do you mean he wouldn't get off his lazy fat back for an old patient?"

"You wouldn't understand," Eliot said. "You're like your father— get the doctor in ten minutes ahead of the undertaker. We of the modern world go in for checkups and cases of sore fingernails, etc. Mostly, we can navigate to the office, but when that isn't possible, the doctor who has made his mark sends an underling who finds it necessary to eat, even when he's just starting out."

"Is this pique?" Bill asked. "Did your doctor, knowing you, refuse to come and view a bellyache of yours in the middle of the night?"

"I'm worried about Irene," Eliot said flatly.

Madeleine smiled at him. "There's really nothing to worry about. Mother always gets this way when she's upset about something."

"What is she upset about?"

"Well, heavens! There's been a murder in the house, and you ask why she's upset!"

"Yes—yes, of course. Well, perhaps I'd better go home."

"For God's sake, go!" Bill said. "I'll phone you after the doctor's been here, to set your mind at rest."

Eliot nodded. "Fine. Let me know if you need me. See you tomorrow, Madeleine. Good night."

He went off, and Bill closed the front door after him with a sigh of relief. He asked Madeleine, "What did he mean, he'd see you tomorrow?"

"I don't know."

"Have you a date with him?"

"Of course not," she said impatiently. "He wouldn't date me. I'm damp firecrackers, as far as he's concerned."

"Well, I don't know." Bill rumpled his hair. "When he first saw you, he began to fizz a bit."

Madeleine laughed. "He'll have changed his mind by now."

"I hope so. I never knew a girl to go for me if he decided to show any interest."

She looked him over. "Maybe Mother's new forthright system *is* working."

"You know very well your mother's only using that excuse to cover her real reason for coming here."

Madeleine dropped her eyes to her twisting hands, and Bill added quickly, "Don't be upset about it. It can't be too serious."

"I know it isn't really serious. It can't be, because Mother could *never* have shut Mrs. Goodhue up in that box."

"Of course she couldn't."

"But who did?"

She sounded a little hysterical, and Bill urged her into a chair. "Sit down now and take it easy. I don't know who did it. Mrs. Reilly wouldn't have had the strength, and her son was ill in bed on the top floor. I feel certain that Eliot would not have been so stupid, and nor would Irene. It would have been a perfectly senseless thing for you to have done. You have your own career shaping up nicely."

Madeleine swallowed. "So nobody did it."

"Well, it had to be someone. Someone from outside, perhaps, or I did it myself."

Madeleine palmed her damp eyes and gave a shaky little laugh. "I expect you had the best reason. She was up to something, apparently, and you should know her better than anyone. She's been around for ages. She was here before Mother and I left."

"She kept her mouth shut," Bill said. "And I'll admit that I never gave her much thought."

The doctor arrived, and Bill went upstairs with them and waited outside the door. When they emerged again at last, the doctor was saying, "Just a stomach upset. I think she'll sleep until morning now."

"She hasn't been out today," Bill said. "How could she have a stomach upset?"

The doctor gave him a chilly glance and said, "Here's a prescription, if she has any more trouble through the night."

Madeleine took the piece of paper and looked down at it rather helplessly, and Bill said, "Where can we get it filled now? It's too late."

"Oh. Yes. Where's your phone? I'll have it sent over. You'd better wait up for it."

When the doctor had left, Madeleine turned to Bill and said, "You'd better go to bed, I'll wait up for the medicine. You have to get up in the morning, and I don't."

"No, I'll wait with you. You don't want to hang around here alone after what happened last night."

She shivered and gave him a grateful glance. "Thanks, Bill."

He shrugged. "I couldn't sleep, anyway."

"I know. Mother took some of her sleeping pills earlier, but it was no use. She couldn't even stay in bed. She went out into the hall once and thumbed through the telephone book. She didn't phone anybody, she just wrote down an address. She was so ill afterwards that she could hardly get back to bed."

"Where's the address she wrote down?" Bill asked.

"Does it matter? I have it here. She told me to put it in her purse."

Bill looked at it and felt his scalp prickle. It was the same address that Mrs. Goodhue had written on the telephone book.

Chapter Eighteen

BILL MUTTERED UNDER HIS BREATH, AND MADELEINE ASKED quickly, "What is it?"

"Mrs. Goodhue had written this address down, too. No name, in either case. I'm going there first thing in the morning."

"Why don't you hand it over to Dykes, first thing in the morning?"

"No—I—no, I don't think so."

Madeleine nodded. "Mother, of course. I could wring her neck, getting mixed up in a thing like this. There's no need for it. It's stupid!"

"Don't worry about it," Bill said kindly. "Apparently it was Mrs. Goodhue's pipe dream, and she involved the Reillys, and Irene, too, I suppose."

Madeleine sighed. "I don't see what she could have to do with it. It seems to be all about a resemblance between you and Mrs. Reilly's son."

Bill nodded. "But do you remember that last question Dykes asked Irene? Were there any lights on downstairs when she went to throw the hair away?"

"Well?"

"She wouldn't have gone all the way downstairs just to throw my curl away. She could have flushed it down the toilet, or several other things, like throwing it out the window. Actually, she went downstairs to meet Mrs. Goodhue. She slipped up when she told Dykes that lights were burning downstairs in the middle of the night."

Madeleine stared at him. "But that makes it much worse. She

went down to meet Mrs. Goodhue, and the next day Mrs. Goodhue is found murdered. Oh, Bill! this is awful!"

"No, it isn't," he said quickly. "You know your mother wouldn't do a thing like that. She had a date with Mrs. Goodhue and she went down to keep it with the curl clutched in her hand. Now Mrs. Goodhue had already gone to the trouble to put water in my lotion so that the curl would stick up and impress Mrs. Reilly with my resemblance to her son. Irene comes down with the curl to confound Mrs. Goodhue, but Mrs. Goodhue isn't there. So she throws the curl into the garbage pail."

Madeleine shook her head a little. "You're nice, Bill, but if Mrs. Goodhue didn't keep the appointment, Mother would hang onto the curl to show her later."

"I don't see why. Mrs. Goodhue would see me in my shorn state the next day, anyway. There was no need to keep the curl."

"Oh, I don't know." Madeleine ran the back of her hand across her forehead. "I'm all confused. Maybe they did meet, and Mrs. Goodhue threw the curl away after Mother left."

There was a sound of rustling at the head of the stairs, and they both looked up.

"Madeleine," Irene called. "Are you down there?"

"Mother, you should be in bed. We're waiting for some medicine to be delivered for you."

"Well, dear—" Irene put a delicate white hand on the bannister. "I'm better, but I'm damned if I can sleep. I'm coming down."

Bill started up to try to dissuade her, but she put him gently aside. "Darling, I cannot stay in that room any longer. I must walk around. I'm much better, though. I suppose I must have eaten something that disagreed with me."

She headed for the library, and they followed her. Madeleine said, "No more liquor, Mother."

Irene had been groping for the light switch and she said irritably, "My dear, you are the damnedest bore. So *stuffy!*"

"Yes, I know."

Bill turned on the light and helped Irene to a chair. Her gold robe flowed gracefully around her, but there were dark smudges under her eyes.

"Perhaps some warm milk," Bill said firmly, "or a cup of tea."

Irene rested her head against the back of her chair and closed her eyes. "What have you done with Eliot? Driven him home to his own liquor cabinet? I don't like to be rude, but I really can't stand you two just now."

Madeleine sat down beside her. "Liquor isn't going to help you, Mother, or even milk or tea, but you'd feel infinitely better if you'd just tell us all about it. You're always ill when you have things on your mind."

"Darling you sound like a clinic, or something—so dull, no elegance at all. I really did my very best for you, too. I worked hard over you."

"It serves you right," Madeleine said. "You went and married Smith, and now you have the nerve to blame me because I take after him."

"I know, dear, I know that Smith was simply *frightful*. He was *always* right, as you are, too, dear. A man can sometimes get away with it, but a woman, *never*. I haven't been able to marry you off. I never will, and I apologize. I should never have married Smith—such a decent man, though—but here you are, and what chance have you for any happiness?"

Bill couldn't help laughing, and Madeleine said, "Ah, shut up, you dullard. You'll marry a lump of wood like me, someday, and turn out solid, wooden little kids who are always right."

"Darling, for God's sake don't insult him!" Irene exclaimed. "He's perhaps your last chance." She glanced up at Bill and added, "She really is a pet, you know, so *very* worthy."

Bill dropped into a straight chair, and folding his arms along the top, looked directly at Irene. "You don't have to tell me whether Madeleine's a pet or not. I can find out for myself. But I do know one thing. You did not come here to try and make a match between her and myself."

"I believe I'll go back to bed," Irene said faintly.

Bill shook his head at her. "You wouldn't be able to sleep. You must tell Madeleine and me all about it. We're for you, you know, and Dykes isn't here. We think that perhaps you've been foolish and mistaken, but nothing more. Now tell us."

Irene carefully arranged the gold robe into smooth folds.

"Come on, Mother," Madeleine urged.

Irene brushed back hair from a white brow and sighed. "Oh, dear. it's all so absurd, and awful. I don't know whether I'm in a mess or not."

"We could help you to decide," Bill suggested.

"Well, dears, here goes, although I ought really to keep quiet, because it's quite possible that the thing has died with Mrs. Goodhue. But it keeps running around in my head, and I feel as though I shall go crazy with it. You know, Bill, when I left your father, it was because I had fallen in love with somebody else. Your father was always very decent. I went to Paris and wrote him about it from there, and suggested that he get a divorce. I could not afford it myself, and neither could my friend, who was my only mistake. Your father wrote and told me, after a while, that he had the divorce, and sent me a nice sum of money. He didn't have to do that, of course, but as I say, he was decent. I never did marry the other one. He showed up too badly, and that saved me plenty, too. I married someone else in a huff, someone with money. Well, anyway, there's no need to go into all that. But a while ago I received a letter from Mrs. Goodhue telling me that your father never had gotten that divorce, that he didn't want to go through the proceedings, and that she could prove it. She said if I didn't come back and arrange to stay in the house for a while, she'd notify my two subsequent husbands, who could then demand the money they'd settled on me. She also mentioned bigamy, quite nastily."

"But surely you could find out whether there had been a divorce or not," Bill interrupted.

"Well, I did try and I didn't find any trace of it, but it was all so difficult because I didn't want to take anyone into my confidence."

"I'll look into it for you," Bill said promptly. "Do it through a lawyer. Didn't he send you any papers or anything of that sort?"

"No, just a letter telling me I was free, and a nice check."

"And you accepted that?"

"If you mean the check, darling—naturally. If you mean your father's statement, of course I accepted it. He was so solid—a rock. I never knew him to tell a lie."

Bill laughed a little. "He never lied unless it was really necessary, and then he was always believed because of his reputation for truthfulness. I suppose he thought it was a good way out, although he must have realized that you could always claim a third of the business, as his wife."

Irene put a hand on his arm. "But, darling, don't you see? A third of your nice little business would not be nearly enough to compensate for what I'd have to return to those two men. *That* was Mrs. Goodhue's threat."

"I don't get it."

"Well, neither do I, actually. As soon as I got here, Mrs. Goodhue talked to me. She told me that Mrs. Reilly would be here that afternoon and I was to hire her. She would leave, pretending to be annoyed, and then come back as soon as Mrs. Reilly was in. She said Mrs. Reilly would be here before you got home, but she wasn't."

"No, she was too late. She and I were on the same subway train. I suppose she followed me and realized who I was, so she had to come back the next day."

"Oh. Well, anyway, I asked Mrs. Goodhue what she thought she was doing, and she told me to keep quiet and that within a week everything would be all right."

Bill and Madeleine sat looking at her, and she gave them a little pout.

"Such a horrid woman, so unpleasant. But, oh, I do wish she'd stop walking up and down those back stairs."

Chapter Nineteen

BILL LOOKED A LITTLE STARTLED, BUT MADELEINE WAS merely annoyed. "Mother! Stop being dramatic! It's not the time or place for it."

"It may be a blow to your superiority, darling, but I am *not* being dramatic. Mrs. Goodhue is walking up and down those back stairs—up and down, up and down. It's not for us to try and explain these things. It's her spirit, and it walks in vengeance. She *never* forgave me, you see. It was when I lived here—I was young, and she was a servant, and it seemed right to me. I told her she must use the back stairs. We got on well enough otherwise. She loved money, and I gave her extras, but she simply *never* forgave me for that affront to her dignity, telling her to use the back stairs. Darlings, I can't sleep up there. She keeps going up and down, up and down, and she'll never stop!"

Madeleine caught and held the agitated white hands and said, "Mother, please!"

Bill stood up. "I'll find out who's going up and down the back stairs."

He left the room and made for the rear of the house. The back stairs ran from just outside the back sitting room up to the third floor, with a landing on the second floor, and he knew that Mrs. Goodhue had never used them. In fact, as far as he knew, they were never used by anyone.

In the kitchen he hesitated before two doors, uncertain for a moment which one led to the stairs. He remembered almost immediately and pulled at the right-hand knob, but the door was locked. He tried the other one, which swung open to reveal a closet, but the first door remained firmly locked, and there was no key.

He went out to the front hall, where he met Madeleine. She asked, "What is it?" but he ran on up the stairs and called over his shoulder, "I'm going to find out if that fellow, Joe, has been up to anything."

On the second floor he tried the door that led to the back stairs landing and found that locked, also, and went on up to the third floor. The stairs ended here, but there was a landing and a door, and that, too, was locked. He glanced around and then hurried to Joe's door, where he went in without knocking and switched on the light.

Joe reared up from the bed and let out a thin scream.

"It's all right," Bill said hastily, "only me. I thought you might be downstairs, on the back stairs, I mean."

"What? What is it? What's the matter?" Joe struggled out of bed and stood revealed in Eliot's pajamas, which were much too big for him.

Bill repressed a spasm of amusement and asked seriously, "Have you been using the back stairs?"

"Back stairs? What on earth do you mean? I didn't know you had any back stairs."

"Well, I'd like to look around the room here for the key to one of the doors. It seems to have been mislaid and I want to get in back there."

Joe said, "Of course. Go ahead," but he looked utterly bewildered.

Bill went through the empty drawers of the bureau and looked under the pillow, but there seemed to be nowhere else to search, unless he lifted the mattress and raised the carpet. He was beginning to feel a bit foolish and he said, "All right, Joe. Go back to sleep," and left the room, closing the door behind him. He heard Joe crawl back into bed, and then out again to switch off the light, and in once more.

He went downstairs and found Madeleine still in the front hall. As he breezed by her, she asked, "What's going on?" and he called back, "Nothing. I've merely worked up an appetite for breakfast."

He went down to the kitchen and moved over quietly to Mrs. Reilly's door. It was slightly ajar, and inside there was darkness, but not quiet. Mrs. Reilly was snoring vociferously.

He gave up at that point because he hadn't the heart to wake her. He went slowly up the stairs again, and as he reached the hall, there was a knock on the front door.

Madeleine came out of the library. "That must be the medicine."

They went to the door together and opened it to reveal, not the medicine, but Eliot.

He inclined his head. "Good evening. So nice to see you again. It's been so long."

"That's funny," Bill said coldly, "it hasn't seemed long enough to me."

Eliot came in and closed the door behind him. "There is a very gay party going on at my place. They wished me to join them, but of course I couldn't consider anything of the sort. Had you not expressed a desire for my company at the office tomorrow? Bright and early? I closed my ears and trotted back here. You have a nice large sofa in that back sitting room, and I should like to rent it for the night. Please don't let me disturb you. I can find my way."

"Haven't you the price of a hotel?" Bill demanded.

"Frankly, no. I was surprised and pleased to discover that you were still up. You usually go to bed so depressingly early."

"How did you know that we were still up?"

"I could see your lights from the bedroom window in my apartment. I knew I'd get a better rest here, so I ran all the way."

"Isn't your tenant supposed to be out of your apartment by Sunday night?"

"Well, yes, but it depends upon a definition of Sunday night. Surely you have seen me, occasionally, on Monday morning, looking hollow-eyed and sleepy?"

Bill said, "Not occasionally. Always."

Irene peered out from the library and cried, "Eliot! Darling! I thought I heard your voice."

Eliot swung around. "My dear, you're better!"

"Of course I am."

Madeleine stepped in and said firmly, "That's fine, Mother. We'll go to bed and not bother to wait for the medicine. It should have been here before this, anyway. I'll sleep in your room, on the sofa, so that you won't be nervous. These men must have their rest, too. They have to be up early in the morning."

Bill agreed heartily and declared that he'd leave a note on the door to take care of the medicine. He urged Madeleine and Irene up the stairs, gave Eliot a brief good night, and went up himself. When he was nearly at the top, he paused and looked down at Eliot, who was still standing in the hall. "If you *want* to sleep in with me, I suppose you may."

"God, no!" Eliot said fervently and moved towards the back of the house.

Bill slept restlessly, and was up at six o'clock. He belted himself into a robe and went down to the kitchen to get a cup of coffee. Mrs. Reilly was still snoring, and he made the coffee and was sipping it at the kitchen table when Eliot walked in.

Bill looked him over. "Have you ever seen this hour of the day before?"

"Have you ever tried to sleep on that sofa in your sitting room?" Eliot countered. "Give me some coffee, or order an ambulance."

They had nearly finished their coffee when Mrs. Reilly came limping out in her nightgown. "Well! I didn't know you boys got up so early. Why didn't you tell me?"

"I usually have breakfast at seven thirty," Bill said. "It was just that I couldn't sleep."

"Well, I declare! Now you go on up and get dressed, and I'll fix a nice breakfast for you. Is there anything special you'd like?"

"No, no," Bill said carelessly. "Anything at all."

"There are certain things that I should like," Eliot interposed quietly.

He knew that neither of them would give him any attention, but he carefully described the breakfast that he wanted. When he had finished, Bill had disappeared, and Mrs. Reilly was at the stove. She seemed unaware of him, and he shrugged and went off to get dressed.

Bill came down for his breakfast at seven and found Madeleine and Eliot waiting for him. They were all eating in comparative silence when Joe appeared and said uncertainly, "Good morning."

They greeted him, and Bill added, "Sit down, Joe, and have some breakfast."

Joe perched himself uneasily on a chair, and Mrs. Reilly presently came in, and stopped short at the sight of him.

"Oh, Joe. What are you doing here? You should be in the kitchen."

Joe flushed to the roots of his hair, and Bill said hastily, "I asked him to sit down and have some breakfast with us, Mrs. Reilly."

"Well—" She clicked her tongue. "If you say so. But I didn't plan for him. He could easily pick up something for himself in the kitchen."

Joe stuck to his position, and Mrs. Reilly brought him some silverware, still shaking her head. "I hope there'll be enough, that's all."

Joe stood up abruptly. "Never mind, Mother. I feel well enough to go to the office, only I'll have to start now to get there in time." He departed swiftly, his ears showing red.

Madeleine cast a reproachful glance at Mrs. Reilly. "How could you do that to him? You know he's not strong, and he shouldn't go off like that without any breakfast."

"Oh, he'll pick something up on the way," Mrs. Reilly said comfortably.

Bill finished his food quickly and stood up. "If you'll excuse me, I have things to do. Eliot, see that you get in on time this morning."

"Yes, sir, boss."

Bill took a taxi to the address that Mrs. Goodhue and Irene had both written down. The cab drew up in front of a large building, and he got out and stood looking about him. For a moment he was lost, and then he saw a sign which said "Out Patients" and realized that the place was a hospital.

He had mounted the steps and was in the entrance lounge before he remembered that this was the hospital in which he had been born.

Chapter Twenty

BILL'S THOUGHTS BEGAN TO WHIRL SLIGHTLY. HE'D BEEN BORN in this hospital, and he looked exactly like Mrs. Reilly's son. So maybe Mrs. Reilly's son was twins, and he was one of them and only adopted by his father, and Mrs. Goodhue hoped to make something out of it.

He took a long breath and went straight outside and hailed a taxi. He was on his way to Dykes's office.

He told the whole story of the addresses and his subsequent discovery that the place was the hospital in which he had been born. He mentioned the locked doors to the back stairs and Irene's troubled story of footsteps constantly going up and down.

Dykes was all business, and he presently stood up, eager to go.

"I'll be at my office," Bill said. "Be sure and phone me if you turn anything up."

They went out together, and Bill took a subway. He was a bit late by this time, and when he walked into his office, Eliot was sitting there in a comfortable leather chair. His head was back, his eyes closed, and his mouth open.

Bill snapped the sagging mouth shut and asked in a fury, "Can't you find anything to do?"

Eliot came to with a yawn and a mutter. "Wha's that? 'Smatter?"

"Nothing. Shame to disturb you. I hope you had a nice nap."

"It was most uncomfortable. Pity you couldn't get to work on time. I can't get on with anything until you O.K. this."

He thrust a paper onto the desk, and Bill glanced down, wrote hastily, and handed it back. "All right, get going. We're falling behind all around here."

"I shall continue to hold the organization on my aching back," Eliot said. "You'd better phone your inamorata."

"My what?"

"The superb Madeleine. Your feelings about her are obvious. Therefore, I have been keeping myself in the background."

"Don't be a damn fool."

"I regard it as a worthy, suitable match. You could even travel along when she goes on tour with the whistler. I'd be glad to look after the business for you."

"Get going."

"Yes," said Eliot, "sir. But, phone the poor girl. She'd like to hear your voice. Last thing she said to me when I left was to get you to phone her."

"Get out."

Eliot got out, and Bill plunged into his work. He was almost surprised, several minutes later, to find that he had reached for the phone. Maybe she did want to talk to him—only why didn't she phone herself?

Madeleine answered at once. "Oh, Bill, I'm glad you called. I'm having a bit of trouble here."

"What is it?"

"It's Mother. She's ill again. I've had her doctor in, but he says she's all right. The medicine came this morning, and I gave it to her right away, but it seemed to make her worse. The doctor looked at it and told me not to give her any more. She wants another doctor now, and I don't know who to get."

"Well—" Bill considered. "I haven't had too much to do with doctors. You could always call the fellow I had in for Joe, and Mrs. Goodhue. At least he's bright and cheerful."

"All right," Madeleine said, in some relief. "Give me his number and I'll phone him."

Bill hesitated. "He's just starting out, you know. I don't know how good he is."

"It's all right, just so that we have a doctor coming. Dykes is here, fooling around, and Mother wants to be too sick to see him."

"Oh. Then Jerry should be just about right. He'll find something wrong with her."

Bill proceeded to lose himself in his work until, at twelve fifteen, Madeleine appeared in his office.

"Have you had lunch yet?" she asked.

"No. It's early, isn't it?"

She nodded. "I didn't want to miss you. I had to get away from Dykes, *and* Mrs. Reilly. She's walking around after him, making his life a misery, and she kept calling me, every now and then, to come and watch."

"What on earth is he doing?"

"He took a lot of fingerprints and then he went to the library and was going through all the papers in the drawers, in the desk and that chest."

"What right has he to do that?" Bill said indignantly.

"I don't know, I'm sure. I had to get out, so I told him I had a date with you for lunch. He'd tried to stop me and make me stay there, and when I told him I had a date, he insisted on knowing who the man was. When I said it was you, he let me go, but asked me to come back as soon as possible."

Bill nodded. "We'd better not make a liar out of you, then. Shall we go to lunch?"

She laughed a little and said, "No hurry about it, if you're busy."

"What about Irene?"

She laughed again. "That Dr. Jones of yours is perfect. He's going to stay with her most of the day. Says he's a new type— medical psycho, or something like that. Anyway, he's going to stick around for hours until he gets to the root of her trouble. When I left, he was preparing to go down and mix cocktails for them and tell Mrs. Reilly what to prepare for lunch."

"Are you sure it wasn't Eliot with a beard on?" Bill asked.

"No, no beard, and not Eliot."

Eliot appeared at the door as she finished speaking and murmured, "I do beg your pardon." He started to back out, waiting to be stopped, but as they merely stared at him, he came back in and dropped a sheaf of papers on Bill's desk.

"So gauche of me, but I must have your opinion of this, Mr. Runson."

"Has Mother bullied you into doing her work for her?" Madeleine asked.

Eliot gave her a charming smile. "Not exactly, my dear. Actually, I am grinding an ax of my own. It has occurred to me that he might be more human if he were married."

"And you'd push him into any old marriage just to further your own ends?"

"Darling!" said Eliot. "What an odd thing to say! I felt, most deeply, that you were for me, but I nobly stepped aside for his sake. It would have been pitiful had I not done so, he fell for you with such a resounding crash."

Bill, looking over the papers, said flatly, "You've made a mistake here."

Eliot glanced at him. "Yes, usually." He turned back to Madeleine. "Bill is a fine, steady man. A little careful of the money, perhaps, but he represents security, rocklike security. I believe a girl like you could get things out of him."

Bill gathered up the papers and said, "Correct the mistake and get this off. You came in here to snoop. You have snooped, so get going."

Eliot got going, and Madeleine wrinkled her nose. "Do you know something? He was crude."

"He's always crude."

"Oh, no." She shook her head. "Very well polished, as a rule. He was trying to sicken you of the idea of getting married."

Bill looked at her. "I believe you're right. Nothing makes a bachelor madder than people telling him he should get married."

"I'll tell Mother on him."

Bill stood up. "Come on. Let's get some lunch."

Eliot, prepared with hat and coat, saw them start out and managed to make the same elevator. "Where shall we go for lunch?" he asked cheerfully.

"Who's 'we'?" Bill snapped.

"Well, could it be that you don't want me?"

"It could."

"But you're always willing to lunch with me if I'm around."

"Not when I have a date with a girl."

On the ground floor, Bill took Madeleine's arm and marched her across the street to a restaurant that he often used. The hostess, glazed over with peroxide and black satin, murmured, "Three?" and Bill saw that Eliot was still with them.

"No. Two."

The hostess seated them, and presently led Eliot to a table that was immediately adjacent.

Bill glared, and Eliot quietly ordered a cocktail, after which he discovered Bill with a great deal of pretended surprise. He leaned over and extended his hand. "Well, such a surprise—so delightful. Madeleine Smith and Bill Runson. I was just hoping that I'd run into some friends—lonely, you know."

Bill ignored the hand and turned to Madeleine. "We'll have to talk in whispers, that's all."

"Have we anything to say that he mustn't hear?"

"I don't know," Bill admitted, "but I don't want him to hear it, anyway."

"Lower," Eliot said from his table. "I can hear that."

Madeleine glanced over at him. "I'd like a cocktail," she told Bill. "The same color as the one Eliot has. It's pretty."

Bill raised his eyebrows. "A cocktail for lunch?"

"Oh, God!" Eliot moaned softly. "What a hick you are! You'll never get her this way. In fact, I'm afraid you'll never get her, period."

Bill ground his teeth together and then spoke through them. "Madeleine, will you marry me?"

"Certainly."

Eliot wavered on his chair. "I believe I could be knocked over with a feather."

Bill nodded at Madeleine. "Good. We'll run around and get a ring for you."

"The five-and-dime?" Eliot suggested. "Or the hardware store on the corner might have something."

"The cigar store," Bill said, still through his teeth.

"But of course—the cigar store. May I have the cigar after you have removed the band?"

"No. I'm going to save it for a keepsake."

Eliot's attention had wandered, and he was staring at the door. He said, in an entirely changed tone, "Here he comes, Bill."

Bill looked up and saw Dykes wending his way through the tables. They watched him in silence until he reached them, and he looked directly at Bill.

"Mr. Runson, Mrs. Reilly tells me that you are her son."

Chapter Twenty-One

BILL COLORED DARKLY AND SAID, "THE WOMAN IS A BIT deranged. I am not her son."

"Can you furnish proof of the fact that you are not her son?"

"Why the devil should I furnish proof of anything?" Bill demanded angrily. "You show me proof that I am her son!"

"Yes," Dykes said, undisturbed. "I'm trying to give you a chance. You must have some papers around that would help."

"I have my birth certificate."

"I'll want more than that, and I want it in a hurry. I'll drop by this evening at about six."

He turned around and made off, and Madeleine whispered, "This is awful!"

"I'll take care of the business this afternoon, Bill," Eliot offered. "You can spend the afternoon establishing your identity."

"Why the blue blazes should I?"

"It won't do any harm," Madeleine said pacifically. "Get it done quickly and stuff it down his throat."

"Of course," Eliot agreed seriously. "You can see that he means business, that he believes Mrs. Reilly for some reason. Seems stupid."

"Well, I can't leave the office this afternoon, and that's flat," Bill declared.

"Oh, fine!" Eliot nodded. "Come into the office this afternoon, and then stay away for a day or a week because you're in jail."

"If you'll tell me how Dykes can clap me in jail because Mrs. Reilly says I'm her son, I'll be glad to hear it."

"It's simple." Eliot ran a thoughtful finger around the base of

117

his cocktail glass. "Mrs. Goodhue was murdered, so perhaps you found out that she'd brought Mrs. Reilly around to start something. You look just like her son, so maybe she was in the hospital at the same time as you were born—only you died, and Mrs. Reilly sold your mother one of her twins to be you. Dykes has certainly dug up something. He must have been nosing around in the hospital."

"Of course he was nosing around. I called him and told him. But as for that plot you just expounded, I think you're deranged, too."

"It all sounds very silly, doesn't it?" Madeleine sighed. "But I'm afraid you'll have to get busy and prove you're you. It seems likely that Mrs. Reilly *was* at the hospital when you were born."

Bill stood up. "You can take over this afternoon, Eliot. That Sawyer is coming in, and if you muff it, I'll kick you out into the snow. I mean it. I'm going home and dig up what I can. Are you coming, Madeleine?"

She nodded, and as they started off, Eliot called, "Please! Just a moment. This is very mortifying, but I am temporarily embarrassed, and you have not paid your check."

Bill wrenched a note from his pocket and flung it down. "Here, and don't forget to give me the change."

He was still muttering as he pushed Madeleine into a cab at the door. "Never has a penny on him. I think he does it on purpose so that he won't be called on to spend money on anyone else, and he calls *me* tight! Puts every cent on his back and down his gullet—"

"Oh, shut up!" Madeleine said. "You have something much more serious to consider. Do you think Dykes would have asked you to prove your identity if it could have been done easily?"

"I don't understand why he asked me to prove it at all."

"He said he was giving you a chance. Perhaps the hospital records are faulty, or the attendants dead or disappeared."

"Something like that," Bill agreed. "So I'm got going to bother with them."

"What are you going to do then?"

"I'm going to choke the truth out of that old fool, Mrs. Reilly."

When they reached home, the house was quiet, and Bill started purposefully towards the back hall. Madeleine followed more slowly and said, "Bill, think it over. You'll get more out of her if you take it quietly. She'll only close up and get stubborn if you start shouting."

He nodded impatiently. "Yes. All right. I won't show any annoyance."

He went on down and found Mrs. Reilly in the rocking chair, moving slowly back and forth and humming to herself. When she saw Bill, she started to get up, but he motioned her back.

"It's all right. Don't get up. I want to talk to you."

She gave him a little smile and settled back, and he swung a chair around and sat down opposite her.

"Have you always lived in Brooklyn, Mrs. Reilly?"

She set the rocker in motion with the toe of her foot and nodded. "I always did."

"I suppose you like it there?"

"Oh, yes. It's my home."

"Did you marry a Brooklyn man?"

Her expression became a little severe. "Reilly was a Brooklyn man, all right, but he was no good."

"Why?"

"He left me."

"Oh?" Bill raised his eyebrows. "I see. He left you when the children were young?"

"Joe was about nine," she said, "but the little one was only three."

Bill frowned and shook his head. "Did he ever help you to support the children?"

"Oh, once in a great while he sent over some money, but not often."

"You knew where he lived, then?"

"Not exactly, no. But mostly you could find him at a saloon. I didn't like going into those places, so I just got a job. The boys lived with my sister, but I saw them all the time. She died pretty soon, but Joe was old enough—" She paused, and her eyes seemed to be looking at something very far away. "And then my poor little one—"

"How long did you know Mrs. Goodhue?" Bill asked.

"Oh, for quite some time. That Dykes has been asking about her all day long. I'm tired of hearing her name."

"Is your husband still living?"

"No," said Mrs. Reilly.

"Why did you come all the way to Manhattan when your younger child was born instead of going to a local hospital?"

The rocker slowed to a stop, and Mrs. Reilly began carefully to pleat her skirt. "I don't know," she said presently.

"It was a long journey. Are you sure you did?"

"Did what?"

"Come all the way to this neighborhood when your younger boy was born."

"Boys," said Mrs. Reilly quietly. "Twins, they were, and one was stolen from me."

"How do you know you had twins and that one was stolen?"

"Mrs. Goodhue told me."

"Did you tell Dykes that Mrs. Goodhue told you this?"

Mrs. Reilly raised her chin. "I told him I had twins because I did, and one was stolen from me."

Bill let a moment pass. "You told Dykes that you are my mother."

"I am, dear."

"Well, I want the address of your son, Joe."

Mrs. Reilly gave it and then suggested that Bill have a cup of tea with her. He shook his head, pleaded a recent lunch, and went back upstairs.

The phone was ringing, and it turned out to be Dykes. He said abruptly, "I'm going to Brooklyn and I want you with me. I've been talking with the Reilly's neighbors."

"Well," Bill said indifferently, "you get paid for it."

"Yes. Now, I want to talk with Mrs. Reilly's husband."

"She's a widow."

"I have his address," Dykes went on blandly, "and it isn't a cemetery. One of the neighbors had known her for a long time. She tells people she's a widow for the sake of the children."

They went to Brooklyn on the subway. They left at about four o'clock, but they did not unearth Mr. Reilly until nearly eight. He was asleep in a furnished room and was somewhat the worse for liquor.

"Wotcha want?" he demanded, peering suspiciously.

"Just a few words with you," Dykes said, stepping into the room.

"Who asked *you* to come in?"

"Official business. Police."

Reilly seemed to sober and sag at the same time. He muttered, "I ain't done nothin'."

"No. We just want a few words with you."

Reilly drooped onto the side of the bed and mumbled, "Just a few thousand words, if I know you guys."

"I want some information about your wife."

Reilly raised bloodshot eyes and said cautiously, "Yeah? What's she want now? I ain't got no money. She's the one got it, pilin' it up in stacks. What's she want from me?"

"Nothing," Dykes said. "You are the husband of Mollie Reilly and the father of Joe and Edward Reilly, Edward now deceased."

Reilly looked down at his shaking hands. "Yeah, poor Eddie. He's gotta go, and that other stinkin' little priss still walkin' around with his pinkie finger stickin' out. Joe—named after *me*. Enough to make a guy puke."

"Why did you take your wife to uptown New York for the birth when Edward was born?" Dykes asked. "Why didn't she go to a local hospital?"

"Horspital?" Joe Reilly muttered. "Whatcha talkin' about, anyways? That little Eddie come before the doctor, right at home there."

Chapter Twenty-Two

THERE WAS A SILENCE, AND THEN BILL ASKED, "WAS EDWARD twins?"

Reilly raised his head and looked up at him. "You're stewed, huh?" His eyes focused, and he frowned.

Dykes said, "Now, your wife said she had twins born at that time."

"Who in hell are you talkin' about?" Reilly muttered. "Mollie, or some other dame?"

"I believe we are talking about your wife," Dykes said. "You had a son, Joe, and a son, Edward, now deceased. What work has your wife been doing all these years?"

"Housework. She made plenty and she can have it. You wouldn't catch me bein' a servant to nobody."

"It's possible that she needed money for the boys," Dykes said coldly.

"Ahh, them boys was all right. I sent money."

"Your son, Joe, speaks and dresses well, lives at a good address, and has a better job than you. Perhaps, unlike you, your wife thought more of her boys than herself."

Reilly said, "Ah, go get a hymn book." He proceeded to call his son, Joe, a name that was far from polite.

"Are you sure Edward wasn't twins?" Bill asked.

Reilly gave Bill another look and then turned back to Dykes. "What's with this guy, anyways? Why don'tcha take him home and sober him up?"

"Why don't you answer his question? Did Edward have a twin brother?"

"Nah. I was there, and that damn busy sister of Mollie's, and then the doc comes puffin' up the stairs, late like they always are."

"Were you there during the actual birth, in the same room?"

"Where else would I go except hang outa the window? We only had one room. Joe was there, too, whinin' in a corner, which was all he was ever good for. I smacked him a couple, but I couldn't shut him up."

"Could you swear in court that there was only one baby born?"

Reilly divided a quick glance between them, and his face pinched in. "I ain't goin' to no court. The damn' police ain't got nothin' on me. I told you, Eddie come alone. There wasn't no twin. Fine healthy boy, he was, and he shoulda been Joe the second. She coulda called that other one Edward."

"Thank you, Mr. Reilly," Dykes said formally. "I think we've finished here, Mr. Runson."

Reilly more or less slammed the door after them, and when they had reached the street, Bill asked, "Are you convinced?"

Dykes shrugged. "There'll be a lot of checking to do."

They headed for the subway, and Bill said, "Tell me what you found out in the hospital that made you believe the corny story of my being Mrs. Reilly's son."

"At the time you were being born a Mrs. Reilly was in labor and eventually gave birth to twin boys. She was Mrs. Joseph Reilly, but the twins were not named."

"Is there a record of any deaths?"

"Yes, one of the twins died. I investigated further to try to find out whether anyone knew anything of a Mrs. Goodhue."

"Turn anything up?"

"Not yet. The hospital will get in touch with me if they find anything."

They sat in silence until the train slowed for Bill's station, and he said, "Well, so long. I get off here."

"So do I. I'm coming home with you."

"Ah, well," Bill said resignedly. "I keep open house. Visitors always welcome."

They walked from the station, and when Bill had opened the door with his key, he asked courteously, "Which one of the inmates do you want on the mat?"

"Mrs. Reilly, of course."

"Who else?" Bill agreed. "Come on."

Mrs. Reilly was in the kitchen and she turned a face of sorrow on Bill. "I had such a lovely dinner for you! I put it in the oven, but I guess it's ruined."

Bill sniffed hungrily and said, "Bring it out, and fill up a plate for Dykes, too."

Dykes said, "No, thank you," a little stiffly, but Mrs. Reilly filled two plates and then sat down at the table with them.

Bill began to eat at once, but Dykes merely glanced at the food and said, "Mrs. Reilly, we saw your husband."

She was looking at Bill and she asked, "Does it taste good?"

"Fine, but Dykes is talking to you."

"He's been talking to me all day and I'm tired of it."

"You've been telling me lies all day," Dykes said severely.

"*You're* a liar!" Mrs. Reilly declared indignantly.

"I talked to your husband, and he said—"

"*He's* a liar, too," Mrs. Reilly observed.

"Perhaps. But he told us that Mr. Runson is not your son."

Her eyes flashed fire, and she cried, "I guess I know my own son! He *is* my son, and nobody can say he isn't!"

"You didn't go to a hospital when Edward was born," Dykes said quietly. "You were at home, and there was only one baby."

"I suppose you were there?" she said scornfully. "I went to the hospital, and I had twins."

"Is Joe at home tonight?"

"I guess so."

"Did you phone him to see how he is?"

She shook her head. "Oh, no. I guess he's all right."

"Your husband was drunk," Dykes stated.

"He's always drunk."

"Why did you tell me that you are a widow?"

Mrs. Reilly drew herself up a little. "I always say that I'm a widow. See, I don't want anyone to know that the boys' father is a bum."

"Hmm."

Bill said, "Why don't you phone Joe, Mrs. Reilly?"

She sighed and went over to the kitchen phone. She was not there for long, and when she came back, she said briefly, "He isn't home."

Bill frowned. "It's late. He should be home."

"Oh, maybe he went to a movie."

"He isn't well. He wouldn't go out anywhere."

"Well, I suppose." She raised her shoulders indifferently. "He's out somewheres."

Dykes cleared his throat. "Mrs. Goodhue is dead now, so there's no longer any reason for you to say that you went to the hospital to have Eddie."

"Eddie and his twin brother," Mrs. Reilly said firmly.

"Granting that there were twins, you don't have to insist that they were born at the hospital."

"There!" said Mrs. Reilly. "I always knew I had twins that time. They never told me and they sold the other one."

"Do you think Reilly sold the other one?"

She thought it over for a moment and then nodded vigorously. "Yeah. He was the one must have done it. He's like that."

"Maybe it was your sister," Dykes suggested.

"No, no. She wouldn't do such a thing."

"She was there, though. How could Reilly sell one of the twins without her knowing it?"

Mrs. Reilly looked into space and narrowed her eyes. "I bet she took some of the money, and I never would of believed it of her."

"But if she was there, and your husband, too, you were not in a hospital."

She gave him a look of mild surprise. "No," she said after some thought, "I guess I wasn't, not if those two were there. Such a long time ago. It's hard to remember. But"—she nodded her head—"they were twins, and Reilly stole one and sold him, and now I've found him." She gave Bill a fond look.

Bill shifted in his chair and asked, "Where are the ladies?"

Mrs. Reilly was uninterested. "The one is still in bed. Just lazy, she is. The other went out, all dressed up to kill."

Bill stood up. "I think I'll go and see how Irene is feeling."

He went upstairs, and Dykes followed him as far as the front hall, where he announced that he was going home to get some sleep. Bill went on up and knocked gently on Irene's door.

She called to him to come in, and he found her lying in bed, staring at the ceiling.

"How are you feeling?"

"How do I look?"

"Not as well as usual," Bill said cautiously.

"Darling, you are not very observant. I am *much* better."

"Good. Do you want anything?"

Irene shook her head. "That wonderful doctor you sent to me has taught me to rest and to face my troubles so that they will dissolve. And they have—dissolved, I mean. If it is true that your father never divorced me, then I shall simply get a lawyer and straighten it out. And if Madeleine persists in remaining single, then my daughter is a spinster, and I suppose there are worse things."

"Fine!" Bill said heartily. "Now will you tell me one thing before you go to sleep? You wrote the address of a hospital on a piece of paper. Why?"

"Oh, yes." Irene pulled her pillow down under her shoulder. "The day I arrived, I had a conference with Mrs. Goodhue before she left. She told me I was to remain silent."

"You were to remain silent."

Irene sighed. "She told me there was trouble brewing, but she would handle all the details. Said it was too bad for you that you had that black curl at the front of your head. That's why I cut it off. Really, you know, you do sleep soundly with a little sedative like that."

"And yet, *she* must have put the water in my hair oil," Bill said. "What about Mrs. Reilly?"

"I really don't know." Irene stretched her white arms above her head. "Mrs. Goodhue was evidently running the thing. I searched the whole place for my divorce papers, which I *knew* she was hiding from me, but I couldn't find them. I found an address on the telephone book and copied it down, but I lost it."

"Didn't you find anything else?" Bill asked.

She yawned. "No, but I don't need to worry any more. Your father divorced me, all right. Mrs. Reilly brought the papers up to me this afternoon."

Chapter Twenty-Three

BILL FROWNED AT IRENE AND SAID, "MRS. REILLY BROUGHT papers to you?"

Irene pouted at him. "Darling, don't repeat things like a parrot. It's so tiresome. Mrs. Reilly gave them to me and said she'd found them on the floor in the library, near the desk."

"But how could papers of that sort be lying on the floor?" Bill demanded irritably.

"Well, I think it's simple enough. That Dykes man—so odd, that beret—anyway, he searched the entire house most of the day. He went through *all* your private papers in your bedroom and the library, and he's so untidy. I expect he could quite easily have dropped things on the floor. Madeleine said it was really awful. He'd root through drawers and so on, and then just stuff things back any way at all."

"Damned nerve!" Bill muttered.

"Perhaps you could sue, dear."

Bill took a few restless steps and then came to a halt. "I wonder how Mrs. Goodhue found out about there having been a Mrs. Joseph Reilly at the hospital, at that time, having twins?"

"Don't you *remember*, pet?" Irene said. "Mrs. Goodhue could find out anything, and there was that nurse. She took care of me when I had influenza, right here in this house, when I was married to your father."

"Oh." Bill nodded. "Perhaps that simplifies things. It would be natural for Mrs. Goodhue and the nurse to gossip a bit and become friendly, maybe go to a movie together occasionally. So later, when Mrs. Goodhue saw Edward and noticed the likeness, she was able to find out that a Mrs. Joseph Reilly had given birth to twin boys and that one had died, and she decided that she could make something out of it. Mrs. Reilly was easy to manipulate, of course."

"You're so *clever*, Bill," Irene said admiringly. "That clears everything up, doesn't it? And we don't have to worry any more. I can go off with a free mind."

"You're overlooking one small detail. The police seem to have a persistent, vulgar curiosity about who murdered Mrs. Goodhue."

"Oh, darling!" Irene gestured impatiently. "It's all nonsense! She locked herself in that silly box."

"No." But he didn't argue with her. "About time to go to bed, I guess. I hope you have a good night."

"Good night, pet."

In the hall he hesitated, and turned back from his room and went downstairs. He tried the door leading to the back stairs and found it still locked. He did not bother to go up and try the other doors, but went and got some tools and began the job of removing the lock from the door. He was working over it with bent head when Eliot walked down the hall.

"My dear fellow, what on earth are you doing?"

Bill glanced up and said briefly, "I'll have to get the screens up—things like you getting into the place."

"The front door," said Eliot, "was unlocked, and partly open, too, so naturally, I walked in."

"Why don't you go home to bed?"

"I should like to go home to bed, but when my cousin's fiancée is in need of an escort home when it is late at night, my own comfort becomes secondary."

Bill suspended operations on the lock and looked at him. "Oh. You're going to escort Madeleine home?"

"Naturally, since no one else seems concerned about it."

"What about the whistler fellow?"

"You are so unworldly," Eliot sighed. "The great Inavsy would hardly expect to have to see his minions home from work."

"Why not when a girl works late at night, like that? All the married men I know have to take their babysitters home."

"Madeleine's job doesn't carry as much prestige as that of a babysitter."

"If you're going to escort her home," said Bill, turning back to the lock, "why don't you take off and do it?"

"For one thing," said Eliot, "since she's your fiancée, I thought you might offer to go, and for another, it's too early. She still has the last show to do."

"Uh-huh. Here, hold this, will you?"

Eliot took the extended tool gingerly and was instructed by Bill to hold it in the crack of the door. He said idly, "It seems odd that you have to break into your own home this way. Haven't you a key?"

"Of course I have a key," Bill replied coldly. "It's just more fun to open the door this way."

"Yes, of course. Stupid of me. By the way, have you seen your dear one's show?"

Bill swore at his screwdriver and muttered abstractedly, "What are you jabbering about, now?"

"Well, it's interesting. I went around and had a look at the whistler and his beautiful accompanist. Inavsy doesn't know it, but I am convinced that he would get no bookings without Madeleine. Chances are she'll be out of a job, soon, because she played a short solo while the whistler was getting his breath and it hauled in more applause than any other part of the act."

Bill gave the screwdriver several vicious twists and then let it rest for a moment. "Madeleine got more applause than the whistler, eh?" he asked mildly. "Just by playing the piano?"

"I didn't realize that it would excite you so," Eliot said, "or I would have broken it more gently."

"Oh, well—" Bill plied the screwdriver once more. "I used to hear her practice and it was pretty foul, then, but of course she was just beginning."

The lock fell away suddenly, and the door came open with a bounce. The tool that Eliot had been holding fell to the floor, hitting his toe on the way.

"Clumsy fool," Bill commented. "Why couldn't you have held onto it?"

"You'd better see whether the tool is damaged, quickly, to relieve my mind. That my foot may be bleeding matters only if the blood should happen to stain your floor."

"Shut up," Bill said. "Where's the light in here?"

"How the devil should I know?"

"You should. It's where you always used to hide when you got into trouble here."

Eliot said, "Here's a socket, but there's no bulb."

"O.K. Wait a minute."

"Certainly, as many minutes as you lik. I'm here to serve."

Bill brought some bulbs, fitted one into the socket, and turned on the light.

Eliot waved his hands and made a face. "Look at all the dust. Forgotten and rejected by Mrs. Goodhue, evidently. I suppose the lock's been jammed for years, and she couldn't get in."

"Somebody got in. Look at the footprints."

Eliot looked down and raised his shapely eyebrows. "Hmm, so Irene wasn't merely making a bid for attention when she said that someone was running up and down these stairs."

"She didn't say someone. She said it was Mrs. Goodhue."

"The spirit of Mrs. Goodhue," Eliot corrected. "Irene knows the value of drama."

"Someone's been tramping around here," Bill said flatly. "These are new prints. I can't remember when I used these stairs last, and Mrs. Goodhue never used them."

"Or cleaned them, either," Eliot murmured. "And to think of all the fuss she made about the places that showed! It's really very revealing, isn't it?"

"I know you're a fussy housekeeper," Bill said, "but this is pretty obvious. She kept these stairs locked away because she didn't like them. They were a sign of servitude, and she did not consider herself in that class, so she just pretended that they didn't exist."

"Yes," Eliot said, somewhat intrigued. "I never knew that you were good at this sort of thing, but of course you're right. Since the stairs didn't exist, they didn't have to be cleaned. But after she was murdered, she wandered up and down them like the lost soul that she was, and to frighten her murderer."

"Sure." Bill assumed an annoying smile. "But how would the murderer know that it was Mrs. Goodhue pattering up and down?"

"You have a *point* there," Eliot said seriously. "Irene was the only one who knew. I shall go and ask her."

"You shall not go and ask her. She's trying to sleep. You shall accompany me up these stairs while I look for a footprint that's reasonably clear."

"Are you trying to pretend that two are needed for such a job?" Eliot asked. "It's too narrow for us to go abreast. I shall have to follow, twiddling my thumbs. I might as well tell you that I know what you really want. You're scared to go up this dark staircase alone and you're angling for company to boost your morale."

"It is dark," Bill agreed composedly. "Wait a minute, I'll get a couple of flashlights to take us to the first landing, and then I can put a bulb in up there."

Eliot surveyed his nails and sighed deeply. "I shouldn't have come. I might have known that I'd be dragged into something like this."

Bill had already gone in search of the flashlights, and Eliot considered making a break for the library and a life-giving quick one, only he'd have to run downstairs for ice. So what of that? It wouldn't take a minute.

He made a move, and at the same time Bill returned with the flashlights and thrust one into his hand.

"Now, I'll go up first, and you follow, and we'll try to find a perfect print. If I miss one, you might pick it up, so keep your flash pointed down."

"Go ahead. Your wish is my law."

Bill started up, and Eliot followed, but he did not bother to study the steps. The flashlight hung loosely in his hand while he thought longingly of the liquor cabinet in the library.

Before they reached the second floor landing, Bill said suddenly, "Here we are, clear as a bell. Look."

Eliot looked. Bill had his own right foot beside the print, while his left was on the step below.

"It's a man's print," Eliot said. "Not yours, obviously. Smaller, of course. Your foot is the largest clodhopper I have ever seen."

"That's because you stick around with your own effete companions. The high-school kids these days have feet that make mine look dainty."

"An elephant's feet would not make yours look dainty." Eliot stooped and looked more closely at the print. "Joe didn't make this. I noticed his feet. They're quite small, and he wears slightly pointed toes."

Bill grunted. "This isn't a pointed toe, although it isn't particularly rounded, either."

"Dykes must have made it," Eliot said carelessly.

"I doubt that. I don't think he's been here."

"Well—there's something," Eliot frowned, "something on my mind—"

"Must be an unaccustomed weight," Bill said. "Careful it doesn't crack. Look, put your foot up beside the print here."

Eliot complied, and they both stared down.

The foot and the print were exactly the same size and shape.

Chapter Twenty-Four

"MOST INTERESTING," ELIOT OBSERVED. "A FELLOW WITH MY size foot has been here."

"What fellow?"

"I really don't know. I doubt if we've met."

"How about it being you?" Bill suggested. "You didn't go home last night. You were here."

"I believe," Eliot said, "that that's offensive. What would I be doing on your back stairs?"

"What would anybody be doing on my back stairs? Running up and down in order to scare Irene?"

"But that's it, of course." Eliot tapped his lip. "To scare Irene and keep her quiet. Mrs. Goodhue is dead, but someone is running up and down these stairs to warn Irene that she still has a spiritual eye on her."

"If that's the reason it was done," Bill said in exasperation, "then you *must* have done it yourself. Who else would think up anything so stupid, outside of a dumb goat? How could you know your fool footsteps would sound like Mrs. Goodhue instead of, yes. Now I remember. I was trying to think of it a little while ago, but your dull stolidity always distracts me. You should have seen it yourself, but perhaps you've been too close to it for too long. Or perhaps I shouldn't expect it of your clodlike mentality."

"Save it for your own circle of bright boys and girls," Bill said impatiently. "For God's sake, say what you have to say, in words of one syllable."

"Then listen. Don't you remember Mrs. Goodhue's footsteps? She seemed to put the ball of her foot down first—something

134

like that—and the heel followed with a little click. Remember? Click, click, click, unless she was on a carpet."

"Well, yes." Bill nodded. "I know what you mean. She did click her heels in an odd way, but what has it to do with anything?"

"Don't you see? Irene said it was Mrs. Goodhue, although she knew Mrs. Goodhue was dead. Someone was producing that little click."

"I don't get it." Bill rumpled his hair. "Why did you go to the trouble of clicking up and down these stairs like Mrs. Goodhue?"

"*I?*" Eliot said in a voice of outrage. "I have not been on these stairs, until now, since I was a small boy."

"Then I don't see how your footprint comes to be here."

"Let's go on up," Eliot said grimly. "We might find your size somewhere, and that would be conclusive, too."

"All right, but don't smear this print. Walk around it."

"I have no intention of smearing it. I am much too clever a crook. It would make me look guilty."

They went on up and found nothing very clear as far as the second-floor landing. Bill tried the door, but it was locked, and they moved on, Eliot going ahead this time.

They had climbed three steps when Eliot said suddenly, "Here! Look at this!"

Bill peered around him and saw another clear print in the dust.

"That's Mrs. Goodhue's footprint," Eliot said excitedly. "I'd bet money on it. She must have been here before she died."

"Looks like it," Bill agreed. "Come on, we'll see if we can find anything else."

They found one other footprint that appeared to have been made by Mrs. Goodhue, and when they reached the top, they were surprised to find the door not only unlocked, but partly open.

"You're a very feckless sleuth," Eliot commented. "You mess up that door downstairs taking off the lock without bothering to check up here first."

"It's a simple matter to replace the lock."

"Yes, certainly, and that's why you didn't make a check. If one of the doors had been open, it would have spoiled the lovely fun you had taking the lock off."

"Why *do* you talk so much?" Bill asked curiously. "Is it to keep your ears well oiled so that you won't miss any dirt anywhere? Come on, and we'll get one of Mrs. Goodhue's shoes and see if it matches those prints."

There was no problem in selection since Mrs. Goodhue's three pairs of shoes were all sensible black oxfords and appeared to be identical. They took one, and found that it matched the prints perfectly.

When they had replaced the shoe, Eliot said, "Suppose we descend by the front stairs, as gentlemen should. I feel distressingly dusty and unkempt."

"Unkempt," Bill repeated, somewhat fascinated. "Matter of fact, that's the way you look, too. Hey! Wait a minute. Joe had a pair of your slippers, didn't he? They must be in that room."

"The slippers!" Eliot snapped his fingers. "And you're willing to accuse me without a second thought."

Bill led the way into the room lately used by Joe Reilly, and Eliot exclaimed, "Here they are!" and pounced. They were standing side by side under the neatly made bed.

The slipper fitted the print exactly, and Bill gave a grunt of satisfaction. "No need to take them back up. They're yours. You can have them."

"Thanks very much," Eliot said and added, "that little punk! Using my slippers to sneak around the house and frighten Irene."

Bill immediately started preparations for replacing the lock in the door, and Eliot said impatiently, "Can't you let that go for the moment? This is serious. Where's Dykes?"

"He went home to bed."

"Oh, fine! Sleeping while Rome burns."

"Everyone has to sleep occasionally, including me. It's my next project when this is finished."

"Go ahead. Snore loudly, enjoy yourself. And then pick on me when I'm late tomorrow because I had to see your girl home."

Bill had stopped working and was looking absently at the tool in his hand.

"What's the matter? Are you stuck?"

Bill looked up. "Why was that door upstairs open? I'm pretty sure Dykes didn't open it. I think Joe's here, now. He wasn't at home when his mother phoned. He's here, all right. I'm going to find him."

"Why would he come to this dull place?"

"Where else would he be?"

"At the movies with his girlfriend."

"Oh, no." Bill put the tool down. "He's here, and he's up to something. I'm going to start at the attic and work down. You can help me."

Eliot glanced at his watch. "My dear fellow, I should like nothing better, but I've only just time to go and get Madeleine."

"Madeleine is not a cripple or a fool and can get herself home. Come on."

Eliot started wearily to follow, and then Bill stopped. "You go up the front stairs. He might go down that way if he hears us coming up here."

"Anything you say. If I must go up at all, certainly the front stairs are more suitable for such as I."

Bill went all the way to the top and then had to wait for Eliot, who made a more leisurely journey. When he finally appeared, Bill whispered fiercely, "Why don't you hurry up?"

"What's the matter?" Eliot whispered back. "Are you afraid to be alone?"

"No, you goon. I want you to stand in the hall while I search, so he can't run from room to room."

Eliot sighed and murmured, "Carry on."

They had soon finished in the attic and they moved down to the second floor. They did not find Joe there, either, and Bill decided not to disturb Irene, as she seemed to be quiet. They returned to the ground floor, and Eliot remarked, "Of course, he could be running up the back stairs now."

Bill yawned. "I don't care if he is. I've lost interest. We'll search down here and the basement, and then quit. I'll put the lock back on, and you can go after Madeleine."

"Oh. I can. I thought it was all right for her to dodge the perils of late evening alone?"

"I don't know whether *you've* noticed it or not," Bill said, "but the sound of your voice becomes damned irritating after a while."

Eliot trailed after him around the ground floor and then silently followed him down to the basement.

They found Joe sitting at the kitchen table, eating, and Mrs. Reilly was with him. They pulled up two chairs and sat down, and Joe gave them a weak smile. Mrs. Reilly said, "Well, now! What can I get you to eat?"

Bill shook his head. "Nothing, thanks."

"I had to work late," Joe explained. "I came here instead of going home to try and induce Mother to come with me. I haven't given up yet."

"How did you expect to get home?" Bill asked.

Joe colored. "I hadn't thought about it, but the subways do run all night."

"How long have you been here?"

"I just came."

"Do you know what time it is?"

"No."

"Well, if you stay much longer, it will not be worth your while to go home."

Joe stood up, and his ears were red. "I'll go at once."

"Sit down," Bill said sharply, "and finish what you're eating."

Joe sat down and picked up his sandwich in a limp hand, but he made no attempt to convey it to his mouth.

Bill looked at him for a moment and then said, "It's almost one o'clock. You didn't just get here. You've been here for some time. In fact, you've been on the back stairs again, pretending to be the ghost of Mrs. Goodhue."

Eliot said, "What?" and Joe mumbled at his sandwich.

"Your feet are small. First you wore Eliot's slippers on those back stairs, probably spying, and then you put on Mrs. Goodhue's shoes and clicked up and down to scare Mrs. Wisner."

Joe looked up quickly, and the flash of surprise in his eyes convinced Bill that he had made some sort of a mistake.

"I don't even know Mrs. Wisner, so why should I try to frighten her?"

"She was frightened, at any rate."

"Well, there, Joe!" Mrs. Reilly said, shaking her head. "You always were the queer one. Doing funny things, even when you were a little boy."

Joe dropped the sandwich and stood up. His face was white, and his forehead beaded with moisture.

"You always favored Eddie, always. You never had a good word for me! Oh, yes, I'm a fool—a silly, stupid little insignificant fool! I'll live alone. It doesn't matter. I don't care. I'll be alone—"

Bill said quietly, "Steady, Joe."

Joe glanced at him and seemed to pull himself together for a moment, and then he sagged slowly to the floor as a muffled scream came floating down from above.

Chapter Twenty-Five

BILL AND ELIOT MADE A RUSH FOR THE DOOR, AND YET BILL had time to gain the impression that Mrs. Reilly had not heard the scream. She was turning on the gas under the kettle.

They ran straight up to Irene's room and pushed in through the door. Madeleine was crouched beside the bed, clutching at Irene's hand and whispering, "Mother, Mother, what is it?"

Irene lay still, her eyes half closed, and a thin ribbon of blood running down from her forehead, across her cheek.

Eliot raised Madeleine from the floor, while Bill leaned over Irene, a finger on her wrist. Presently he nodded and went out to the phone in the hall, where he put through a call to the doctor. He returned to stick his head in at the door.

"Eliot, stay there until the doctor gets here. I called Jerry and told him to walk in and come right up. Irene will be all right until then. I'm going down to see that Joe doesn't get away."

"All right," Eliot agreed, "but for God's sake, phone Dykes on your way down. Joe's out, anyway. He won't be able to get up and run for a while."

Bill stopped on the ground floor to put in a call for Dykes, but he had to leave a message, since Dykes had gone home. A bored voice assured him that Dykes and the message would be brought together as soon as possible.

Joe was still lying on the floor, but he had begun to stir and mutter. Mrs. Reilly sat on a chair above him, with a cup of tea waiting on the table beside her.

Bill sat down, and Mrs. Reilly gave him a warm smile. "Would you like a cup of tea, too, dear?"

"Mrs. Reilly, we've been through all this," he said soberly. "I am not your son, and you'll have to address me more formally."

Her expression changed for a moment, and then the smile returned. "No one can ever convince me that you're not my son. I'll *never* believe it."

Bill looked down at Joe. His eyes had been open, but when Mrs. Reilly spoke, he closed them again, and his head dropped sideways.

Bill said sharply, "Joe!"

The eyes flew open again.

"Here, I'll help you to a chair."

Joe allowed himself to be established in a chair at the table, and Bill said, "Now, drink your tea. You should make an effort to take your emotions in hand, you know. You let things hit you too hard."

Mrs. Reilly nodded. "Always did."

"Oh, Mother!" Joe said weakly.

Bill glanced at her. "Please keep quiet, Mrs. Reilly. Now, Joe, you're in a spot, and fainting all over the kitchen floor isn't going to help you. What have you against Mrs. Wisner?"

Joe sipped tea. "I hardly know her. I know only that she is living here."

"That isn't answering my question. I want to know why you went into her bedroom a little while ago and struck her on the head."

Joe's face was green and damp. He had a moment of strangling before he cried, "I didn't. I did not! I haven't been anywhere."

"You were on the back stairs."

"Yes. Yes, I was on the back stairs, but that's where I stayed. I ran out into the hall at the top when you got the bottom door open. I was too fussed to wait and lock that upstairs door after me. I came right down the front stairs and into the front room there, and when you both went upstairs, I came on down here. That's all I did. I haven't been anywhere else. I haven't seen anyone, only Mother."

"Who got hit?" Mrs. Reilly asked interestedly.

"Mrs. Wisner," Bill said.

Mrs. Reilly shook her head from side to side. "Tch, tch."

They fell silent, and Joe sipped his tea. Someone came in on the floor above. Bill, who knew it was the doctor, watched Joe stop sipping and glance upwards. Mrs. Reilly did not appear to notice it at all.

"Joe," Bill said presently, "why did you put Mrs. Goodhue's shoes on and walk up and down those back stairs in the way that she always walked?"

The green tinge appeared in Joe's face again, and Bill thought he was going to deny it, but after a moment, he pulled a long breath and put his cup carefully into its saucer.

"I did it to try and get Mother to come home. It was last night, after she had come back here. She knew Mrs. Goodhue was dead, and I thought if she heard those footsteps, she might get frightened and leave."

"Oh, no, dear," Mrs. Reilly said comfortably. "You know I'm not afraid of the spirits, and never was. I've seen plenty of them in my time, too. Maybe that's why I'm not afraid of them."

"Why don't you just leave your mother alone, Joe?" Bill asked. "Why do you need her?"

Joe shut his trembling lips and appeared to be struggling with tears.

"Why haven't you gone out with the girls?"

"What girl would go out with me?"

"Only a few thousand in your own neighborhood," Bill said mildly. "What's the matter, anyway? Did you ever try to get a girl to go out with you? You'd be surprised at how easy it is."

Mrs. Reilly nodded. "That's what I always tell him. It isn't as if he was a girl. A boy can always get a date, no matter what he looks like."

"Yes, but Joe hasn't any trouble of that sort. He's quite good-looking. He'd have no difficulty at all."

"Joe?" Mrs. Reilly looked at her son. "Good-*looking?*"

"It's no use trying to kid me," Joe muttered. "I've seen myself in the mirror. I *have* asked girls to go out with me, and they always refused."

"Of course they refused," Bill said roundly, "because of the way you asked them. They felt that they were supposed to refuse."

Joe raised his eyes with a flicker of interest. "What do you mean?"

"Well, I think you need help, perhaps psychiatric help. I've never known a fellow with so little self-confidence. If you came in and asked me for a job, I'd say no automatically, and yet you can probably do a job very well. How did you land your present one?"

"The war," Joe said. "Everyone so shorthanded. I'm still there. It's a good position."

"Didn't you fight, during the war?"

"Oh, no. I was rejected, of course."

"Why 'of course'?"

"My fainting spells."

"Actually," Bill said, tapping his fingers thoughtfully on the table, "I don't believe you faint at all. I think you just black out because you don't want to face something."

Someone said, "Very interesting," from the direction of the door, and Dykes walked in. "You've been listening to that peculiar doctor you have upstairs, Mr. Runson."

Bill gave him a bleak look. "Suppose you stick to your own particular business, Mr. Dykes."

"Suppose I do."

"How is Mrs. Wisner?"

"She's coming along nicely," Dykes said, without much interest. "She had a severe blow on the forehead, but it's not as serious as it might have been. She's resting, and the doctor is still with her, and her daughter and your cousin are in the library, doing what they usually do in the library. I don't mean reading, of course."

Bill turned to Mrs. Reilly. "Make some coffee—and perhaps some small sandwiches for Miss Smith, and bring them to the library."

"Sure." Mrs. Reilly got to her feet. "I'll make enough for you, too."

"I suppose you want to question Joe," Bill said to Dykes. "I'll leave you to it."

Dykes nodded, and Bill went upstairs to the library. Madeleine was drooping in a chair, wearing a blue and silver chiffon dress, but her hair hung about her face. He thought she looked lovely.

"I'm over here," Eliot said. "In the green chair."

Bill looked at the highball glass in his hand and observed, "You look very natural. Did you tell Dykes about Joe and the back stairs?"

"Yes, and he was infuriated, in a vulgar sort of way."

"When did he come in? I didn't hear him."

"He gumshoed up the stairs shortly after the doctor got here. Of course you didn't hear him. That's his business. I believe they wear special shoes, or something."

"Why was he infuriated?"

"About the back stairs—he says we should have been more explicit, and Irene neglected to mention the footsteps that pattered up and down. I tried to soothe him by saying that we assumed it was a ghost and therefore of no interest to the police department, since ghosts cannot be arrested, or even questioned."

"I don't know why he overlooked those back stairs," Bill muttered. "He was in here all day, went all over the place."

Madeleine raised her head. "He wasn't searching the house, exactly. He went through your desk here, and your bedroom, and he was in the kitchen, asking Mrs. Reilly endless questions. He questioned Mother and me, too, in her bedroom, but after your Jerry got here he had to quit. Jerry said that Mother was too ill for any more of it."

"I've asked Mrs. Reilly to bring up coffee and sandwiches, Madeleine," Bill said. "Thought it might help."

"Thanks. I guess it will."

Eliot sighed and stretched his legs. "I don't want any."

"Who asked you?" Bill demanded. "There's more expensive refreshment in the liquor cabinet for you."

Madeleine was quietly twisting her hands together. "I don't understand it. Mother isn't the kind to make enemies. Who could possibly want to attack her?"

Jerry walked in and announced, "I'm going now. I've been downstairs and told Dykes and the other two that Mrs. Wisner is not to be disturbed in any way whatsoever. She's had a hypo and she should sleep until morning. You three are to stay out, too, understand? She's to be left entirely alone."

"Of course, Jerry," Bill said. "I'll see that she isn't disturbed. Was she able to tell you who attacked her?"

"No."

"She's better, though?" Madeleine asked anxiously.

"Yes, but she's had the hypo, Miss Smith, and if you go in there, you may wake her. I want her to have absolute rest. Good night."

Bill escorted him to the front door and when he came back, Dykes was in the library.

"I'm going now. I've left a man upstairs in the hall to protect your mother, Miss Smith. I'll be back in the morning."

Bill moved to see him to the door, too, but Dykes waved him back. "I know my way out. Mrs. Reilly is bringing up that supper. You'd better clear off a table for her."

Bill nodded, wondering about Joe. He wasn't being hauled in tonight, anyway. Not enough on him, evidently.

Dykes went to the front door, opened it, and closed it with a bang, leaving himself inside. He went quietly up the stairs, and the man in the hall, seated on a narrow settee, raised his head with a questioning look.

Dykes breathed, "Go to sleep now, and make it sound. Don't muff this."

The man nodded and curled himself onto the settee.

Dykes moved silently into Irene's bedroom and lowered himself into a previously placed chair behind the door.

He fixed his eyes on the dim outline of the corpse on the bed.

Chapter Twenty-Six

HE WAS DOING THINGS OUT OF ORDER AGAIN, SKATING ON thin ice, but he didn't care. All they ever did about it was bluster. They wouldn't throw him out, not when he always brought in the goods.

Everybody's fingerprints had been on that old refrigerator,. Anyone could have shut her in there after banging her on the head—make certain that she would die. Couldn't do the same to Irene. Had to hope that the blows were enough, and they were. She'd died without regaining consciousness. Only that young doctor and himself knew about it. Even the man in the hall didn't know. His instructions were to pretend to sleep and to wake up only if Dykes called him.

He felt lousy that he'd let this happen, but he'd had the whole thing wrong somehow. He'd had no idea that this woman was in any danger. She'd been one of the suspects when the Goodhue woman was murdered. It was logical. Mrs. Goodhue had been getting in her hair, forcing her to come here and make a claim for the business, and then hand most of the money over. She'd have had to claim it privately, as any publicity would have destroyed Mrs. Goodhue's hold over her and lost her the money she'd collected from her last two husbands.

So Mrs. Reilly had given Mrs. Wisner the divorce papers this afternoon, claimed she found them on the floor near that desk in the library. Only he hadn't dropped anything when he'd been going through that desk, and there'd been no divorce papers in the desk.

No. It was pretty clear that Mrs. Goodhue had at some time left the divorce papers with Mrs. Reilly so that they would not be found. Probably didn't want to destroy them because she never knew when they might come in handy. Stupid woman. There would always be a record of the divorce. And what about Irene's own papers? Surely she must have received them. The elder Runson hadn't been a slipshod type. Oh, no, Mrs. Reilly had given those papers to Irene so that she could feel easy about it, or perhaps so that she would hurry away. And that sea-green son, making like Mrs. Goodhue on the back stairs so that Irene would be frightened out. Claimed he was trying to scare his mother home, and how could he expect his mother to hear him from down in the basement?

It seemed to Dykes that the still figure on the bed stirred slightly, and when he raised a hand to rub his forehead, it came away wet.

Everything was wrong. He couldn't get it. Irene had to be killed because she knew something. What other reason could there be?

He had a lousy headache. Better stop thinking about it. He wondered what they were doing downstairs. One of them *must* come up and try to finish Irene off. That young doctor had been cooperative, anyway.

Downstairs in the basement, Mrs. Reilly had gone to bed, and Joe was lying on the old-fashioned sofa in the dining room. He was not sleeping. He lay with his hands clenched at his sides and his wide eyes on the ceiling.

Madeleine, Bill, and Eliot were still in the library. Bill was gathering up the coffee cups and piling them on the tray and he said through a smothered yawn, "We'd better get to bed."

Madeleine was staring down at the carpet. "You go. I wouldn't be able to sleep."

"Go on, Bill," Eliot said. "I'll sit it out with Madeleine."

"I'm damned if I'll go to bed and leave you two sitting it out. In the first place, Eliot, you have to be up early in the morning, as you very well know, and in the second place, I wouldn't leave you with Madeleine anyway."

"What about the third place?" Eliot asked in a bored voice. "You're such a crude yokel. She's your girl, yes, but you'll have to leave her alone with other men at some time."

"Some time isn't now."

Madeleine continued to study the carpet. "Shut up, both of you! I'm so worried, I can't see straight."

"Sitting up all night isn't going to help you," Bill said reasonably. "Can't you take one of her sleeping pills? You need rest."

"No. They're in the bedroom with her."

"Well, try a couple of aspirin. They might help you to get off."

Madeleine got out of her chair and began to pace the room restlessly. "Oh, I don't know. I could try, I suppose, but I don't think it would do any good."

"Yes, it will, if you relax with it. Come on upstairs, and I'll get the aspirin for you."

"What about me?" Eliot asked. "Does it matter that I shall not be able to sleep? You could offer me a couple of aspirin, too."

"Don't be a jackass. What good do you think two little white pills would do, floating around in a sea of alcohol?"

"Oh, I see. Of course. If I want aspirin, I'll have to go home and get my own. Wouldn't it be all right if I leave a nickel beside the bottle?"

Bill had an arm about Madeleine and was leading her out to the hall, and Eliot followed lazily.

"Why don't you go home?" Bill asked over his shoulder.

"No. There is trouble in the house, and I have a certain amount of nobility under my silken exterior."

"O.K. Where do you want to sleep this time? In with me?"

"God, no!" Eliot said with feeling. "I'll retire to that couch in the back sitting room again. It will do for a poor relation like myself."

"You're nuts," Bill said indifferently. "You might just as well go home. We have a man upstairs to look out for us."

"I'll just go up to the bathroom," Eliot murmured delicately. "Really, Bill, you should have some facilities down here. It's embarrassing."

He went on up, and Bill followed with Madeleine. He waited for them at the top and then pointed to the man curled up on the settee.

"Observe the way your guardian looks out for you."

Madeleine said, "Hush. We'll wake him quietly."

She went over to the man and touched his arm, and he stirred and sat up. "Eh? What is it?"

"Would you like some coffee to keep you awake?"

"No—no, thanks. It's all right."

Dykes had been listening carefully and he decided that his man had handled it all right. He heard Eliot go along to the bathroom, but Bill and Madeleine lingered, talking to each other in whispers. Eliot came back presently and said something to them, and then they dispersed, Eliot going downstairs, and Bill and Madeleine to their rooms.

Dykes knew they would be out again. He'd had his door open about an inch, and now he swung it a little wider. His man was pretending to be asleep again, and he took a short step over and prodded him. He murmured against his ear, "Too soon. When they come out to go to the bathroom, look sleepy but awake, and then curl up and go off when they retire."

The man grounded his legs once more and assumed what he hoped was a sleepy expression. You sure got some lousy assignments in this job, and that Dykes, like top brass anywheres, oughta be behind a locked door stickin' straws in his hair.

Dykes moved back into Irene's room and tried to pick up his line of thinking, but somehow he couldn't concentrate, not until those two came out and went in again.

Madeleine came first, and when she had disappeared into the bathroom, Bill emerged. Dykes sneered quietly to himself. He'd be there when she came out, and how long would it take them to ask each other how they were? They hadn't seen each other for so long.

Dykes presently went to the door and peered out. They were standing down near the bathroom now, talking in whispers. As he watched, Madeleine moved off to her own room and Bill went into the bathroom. He was there for only a short time, and then he came back along the hall towards his room at the front. He paused at the settee to assure himself that the man was still awake and then moved on again. He switched off the hall light before turning in at his own door.

The darkness was absolute, and Dykes clamped his teeth together in annoyance, but the man on the settee was relieved. Now, he could keep his damn eyes open. He'd begun to feel as though he'd have to use paste to keep them closed.

Dykes returned to his chair behind the door. Somebody would be in to finish Irene off, he couldn't be wrong about it. She'd been attacked because she knew something, not because she was in the way. She wasn't in the way. She had nothing to do with this. The whole scheme had failed. Bill had been able to prove he was not Mrs. Reilly's son. Lousy records that hospital kept, anyway. The mastermind, presumably Mrs. Goodhue, had been foolish in figuring she could work along with a simple woman like Mrs. Reilly. She had expected to control her, though, thought Mrs. Reilly would just act natural when she saw Bill. It wouldn't be hard to convince her that Bill was her son. O.K., but if Bill were her son, then the business should belong to Eliot. So the idea had been merely to blackmail Bill, threaten to expose him if he didn't pay up. And Mrs. Reilly could stay here, too, to satisfy her. Also, she could do a lot of the work. But why was Irene hauled in? Mrs. Goodhue had watered the hair lotion so that Bill's curl would stick up and he would look like Eddie's twin brother, and Irene had gone to a lot of trouble to cut the curl off so that he would *not* look like Eddie's twin brother. An effort to drop the bottom out of the scheme from the beginning by getting Mrs. Reilly to decide that Bill was not her son. So she cut the hair off and *went downstairs*. There was no need to go downstairs to get rid of the curl. She could have done anything with it. She had said, carelessly, that the light was on downstairs,and yet it was the middle of the night and the light should have been off.

She hadn't gone down to see Mrs. Goodhue because Mrs. Goodhue's room was on the top floor, and if they'd had a date to meet in the middle of the night, it would hardly have been within earshot of Mrs. Reilly. No, the chances were that Irene had gone down to see Mrs. Reilly herself. And it was probable that Mrs. Goodhue had already been shut into the box.

Joe had been sleeping upstairs. Perhaps he'd come down again while Mrs. Reilly and Mrs. Goodhue were talking, and then, after his mother had gone to bed, he'd murdered Mrs. Goodhue.

Later on, Irene had come down to try and convince Mrs. Reilly that Bill was not her son.

That was it. Irene hadn't been able to get anywhere with Mrs. Reilly, of course, and she'd written down the address of the hospital so that she could go around and check for herself. Well, the hospital hadn't helped him much. They couldn't produce anyone who had been there at the time, just a few addresses of elderly women who were glad enough to jabber, but couldn't tell him anything.

Well—so after Mrs. Goodhue's death, Mrs. Reilly and Joe had been very anxious to get Irene out of the house and away. One finds her divorce papers, and the other tries to scare her by flitting up and down the back stairs.

Now, about Eliot. The business would really be his if Bill had turned out to be Mrs. Reilly's son. He could get rid of Mrs. Goodhue and take over the control of Mrs. Reilly. He could get rid of Irene, too, and he hadn't left the place. He was still here.

What motive did Joe have, actually? To get his mother home? No. Certainly, he was all twisted up in an effort to get his mother's attention. e'd never had it, or perhaps he'd had it until Eddie was born, but never after that. So he killed Mrs. Goodhue to get his mother back to himself. How could you tell? A fellow all twisted up like that could do almost anything.

Bill. Mrs. Goodhue threatening to turn his life upside down. He'd have plenty of reason to slap her into that box. The girl, Madeleine? Some hangover from her childhood of Mrs. Goodhue's cold meanness. But Mrs. Goodhue had practically brought Bill up, and he hadn't turned out so badly. Why would she plan to mess him up at this stage? Well, of course, she hadn't, really. She hauled Irene in and hid the divorce papers where Mrs. Reilly found them later, and told her to stand by. Bill, who was the kind to give up the business if he did not believe it to be rightfully his, would be told that it would go to Irene and not Eliot, and Bill might think twice about handing it over to Irene. He'd keep it, and his mother, in style, and Irene would go away, and so would Mrs. Goodhue, to live on what Mrs. Reilly sent her.

There was a faint sound from somewhere. Dykes held his breath and then let it out slowly. Just that jerk out there on the settee, probably.

But what a bum plan, to sit by and expect Mrs. Reilly to send money. There wouldn't be enough, and Mrs. Goodhue should have known that. All this trouble for a plan that was basically stupid. Oh, no, it was wrong. Everything was wrong. Dykes saw his mind whirling around with all the different bits and pieces. Irene had figured it out, and now, perhaps, in these last few minutes, so had he.

The proof would come tonight. It must. It would save so much trouble.

The faint sound was repeated, and he almost smiled. This was it.

The door opened without sound, and a figure seemed almost to float in. It was hard to see at first. But there was a finger of light from the window that lay straight across the bed. The figure lifted an arm, and Dykes spoke.

"You needn't do that. You killed her the first time, Mrs. Reilly."

Chapter Twenty-Seven

JOE HAD GONE INTO ONE OF HIS FAINTING SPELLS, ELIOT WAS standing by, but had decided to change the treatment a little. Instead of the usual cup of tea, he held a small glass of whiskey. Madeleine was sitting with her feet up on a chair, balling a damp handkerchief in her palms, and Bill paced the floor of the library in silence. The lamps were still on, but dawn had begun to pale them a little.

Bill paused and said abruptly, "Dykes's explanation of what happened was a bit sketchy. Is Joe still out cold? I want to talk to him."

Eliot turned the glass of whiskey in his long fingers. "You may talk to him, but you won't get an answer just yet."

"Dykes implied when he was leaving that he'd been pretty clever about the whole thing, but I'm of the opinion that he ought to be reported. Irene murdered while he was supposedly sitting on top of the case."

Madeleine's eyes filled again, and Bill moved over to put a hand on her shoulder.

"Here he comes," Eliot said.

Joe moaned and stirred, and Eliot knelt down and raised his head. He poured a little of the whisky into the slack mouth, and Joe choked, struggled, and then blinked around at them quite rationally. Bill and Eliot raised him and put him into a chair, and Bill muttered, "What do you mean by giving him whiskey! I suppose you even clean your teeth with the stuff."

"Tea is nauseating at any time," Eliot said firmly, "and particularly gruesome when you're not feeling well. Anyway, look at him. He's all right."

Joe pulled a palm across his sweating forehead and whispered, "I'm sorry. Where's Mother?"

"She's gone," Bill said sharply, and watched to see whether he'd go off into another faint.

"No! Oh, no!"

"Pull yourself together, Joe. You'll be much better living alone, and I think you know it as well as I do. Now, I want to ask you some things."

"I can't, not when she's in jail, or—or worse—"

"There's a good chance she'll end up in an asylum," Bill said. "She was still pretty vague when she left. You know that vagueness is only an act, don't you?"

Joe nodded miserably, and Bill asked, "When did you last see your brother Eddie?"

"What's that?"

"Come on!" Bill said roughly. "Dykes told me all about it. When did you last see him?"

"Why, he lived. Mother took us to Scotland. I think he was four or five. She left him with some well-to-do relatives. They wanted him and they were to educate him, and she thought it would be a good thing."

"You haven't seen him since then?"

"No, but we always had photographs, and Mother saw him."

Bill nodded. "Are you aware that those were photographs of me?"

"You!"

"Yes. Mrs. Goodhue must have told your mother about the Mrs. Joseph Reilly who had twins at the hospital when I was born, and your mother decided that it would do no harm to pretend that her son Eddie was a twin and I was the other half. Figured maybe she could do something with it."

Joe shook his head from side to side. "Oh, no, no. That's just foolish."

"How many photographs of your brother Eddie did your mother have around the house?"

"Only two. One taken when he was thirteen and the other when he was eighteen."

"Right. So she stole some photographs of me and then showed

them to Mrs. Goodhue—got money out of her."

"Wait a minute," Eliot interposed. "Why would Mrs. Goodhue think they were photos of Eddie? She knew what photographs you'd had taken, and the name of the photographer."

"Yes, but these were enlarged snapshots, weren't they, Joe?"

Joe moaned, "I don't know, I don't know."

"Yes, you do. It's quite possible that Mrs. Goodhue gave your mother a snapshot of herself during the course of their friendship, one with me in it, and she had my head enlarged into a photograph."

"Why didn't she use it before?" Eliot asked.

"She used it from the beginning. You know, if Mrs. Goodhue really cared for anyone, it was my father. I've no doubt at all that Mrs. Reilly told Mrs. Goodhue *she* was the Mrs. Joseph Reilly who had twins at the hospital. One was supposed to have died, but she hinted that it was not her twin who had died. Someone had stolen him from her. The first snapshot she picked up from Mrs. Goodhue was fixed up with an enlargement of my head, and the next time Mrs. Goodhue turned up for a visit, she showed it to her. It's easy to understand Mrs. Goodhue's reaction, and a simple step from there for Mrs. Reilly to mention the resemblance in the snaps and loudly proclaim that I was the twin who had been stolen from her and that she was going to do something about it. Mrs. Goodhue undoubtedly offered to pay her something regularly to keep quiet about it.

"Mrs. Reilly was easily quieted, since she knew that if she did try to claim me there would be an investigation which might include someone taking a look at Eddie, who was not at all like me."

Joe's head hung down and he was moaning softly, and Bill said in sudden fury, "For God's sake, sit up and head into it, and be a man!"

Joe straightened a little and muttered, "I'm not a man in your definition of the word, and never was and never shall be. I'm only a fool."

"You are a fool to let your mother roll you over a barrel like this. You've been jealous of Eddie all these years, and yet your mother let him go and kept you."

"Only because they wanted him. They naturally didn't want me."

"No, naturally. And your mother naturally didn't want Eddie, either. A child of four or five is a pest, any way you look at it. But you were older and could help around the house. Isn't that so? Your mother didn't care for either of you. She merely talked Eddie up to see you squirm. But you never saw Eddie after he was twelve, did you?"

"Not since he was adopted," Joe sighed.

"Why was that? Eddie came over here, didn't he?"

"No. Mother used to go over and see him."

"She never took you?"

"No. But she saw that I had a good education. I went to college." There was a suggestion of fire in Joe's eyes, and Bill glanced at him and then changed his tone a little.

"That was one good thing she did, but she was able to afford it. Working as a servant in the last fifteen years was lucrative, and she had the added income from Mrs. Goodhue."

Joe found no defense and dropped his head again.

"You know that, don't you?"

Joe balled his hands into fists and said, "I know Mrs. Goodhue gave Mother money every week, but I always understood it was for extra cleaning here."

Bill shook his head. "That one won't wash. You told me that your mother had been living with you, and not working, for the last few years."

"She told me she was going off in the middle of the day and coming back early, so that the neighbors would think she was merely on a shopping tour. I begged her not to, but she said she enjoyed it."

"I expect she did, because she really was going shopping or to a movie. I assure you, she never came here. I'd have seen her. Did Mrs. Goodhue bring her the money?"

Joe nodded. "On Saturday nights, except, occasionally, when Mrs. Goodhue was ill. Then Mother would go for it. So she *was* at your house."

"Yes, but I suppose Mrs. Goodhue took care that she never saw me. I know how she felt."

"They were good friends," Joe declared. "I don't see how you can think that Mother was blackmailing her."

"Mrs. Goodhue was not the mean person that people often thought her," Bill said quietly. "She was reserved and not affectionate, but I know very well that she had feelings. She had her charities, and she probably felt that your mother had every right to some compensation for giving up her son. She was willing to pay it to spare my father the pain of realizing that he had no son, and to spare me, after him. She should have investigated earlier, of course. When Eddie died, Mrs. Reilly realized that nobody could stand him beside me and see any resemblance, so she moved forward into an adventurous bid for bigger money. I suppose that's why she showed fear, as well as surprise, when she saw me in the subway. She went home, but *had* to come back the next day and go on with it.

"Mrs. Goodhue realized that she was a traitor and started action on her own behalf. She looked up the address of the hospital and wrote it down on the phone book, and then she went around there and found that the doctor had died and the nurses were more or less out of the picture. She got in touch with Irene and told her to come, said that her divorce from my father had never gone through. Irene came in a hurry, of course, and Mrs. Goodhue hid the papers, probably on her own person. Mrs. Reilly found them there and kept them until it seemed wise to return them to Irene."

"*Why* did she have to drag Mother into this?" Madeleine cried. "It wasn't necessary!"

"Oh, yes, it was," Eliot said. "I believe I can see it now. Just like Mrs. Goodhue. She probably wanted me there, too, for the first time in her life. We all had to be around, everyone who could help Bill and testify that we knew him as Bill Runson. That's why she went to the hospital, to find out if she could get hold of a nurse who had been there, or a doctor. Backed up by all of us, she was going to make a clean breast of everything, including the money she'd been paying Mrs. Reilly."

"That's about it," Bill agreed. "Mrs. Reilly couldn't allow it, of course. She'd been blackmailing Mrs. Goodhue and had figured on her help. She wasn't going to get it, and she knew that a showdown would be fatal. She might have retired at that point and gone home, but the thing had gone too far, and she couldn't stop it. She murdered Mrs. Goodhue, instead. She hit her while she was sitting in one of those kitchen chairs, rolled her over to the box, removed the shelves, and eased her in."

"But why Mother?" Madeleine whispered.

"She didn't know how much Mrs. Goodhue had told Irene. When Irene cut off my hair, she realized that she had some knowledge. I know Irene went down that night for some purpose other than disposing of my hair. She had made a date with Mrs. Reilly to try and find out more, but I don't imagine that she got much out of the interview, if Mrs. Reilly showed up at all. So Irene put the hair in the garbage and went back to bed.

"Later, Mrs. Reilly picked the curl out of the garbage pail and pretended she was keeping it for sentimental reasons. It was the same with that oil painting she took—laying the foundation."

Madeleine took a long, quivering breath. "But didn't Dykes tell you why she turned on Mother?"

"You remember when I cam. Everything was fine. Mrs. Reilly had brought up the divorce papers, and she had had a nice talk with her, and you can guess at the nice talk. Your mother was not slow, Madeleine. She knew very well that Mrs. Reilly had not picked those papers off the floor but had found them somewhere. She must have guessed that the most probable place was Mrs. Goodhue's person, and that Mrs. Goodhue would not have given them up before she died. But Irene never delved much into the right or wrong of things, and it's my guess that she made a deal with Mrs. Reilly to get out and stay out. Irene was not frightened when I saw her. She hadn't thought beyond the fact that Mrs. Reilly would go, and it hadn't occurred to her that since the woman had murdered once, she might easily murder again, especially when it meant getting rid of the person who knew about the first crime."

Madeleine shuddered and pulled at her wet handkerchief, and Bill turned to Joe.

"Why did you run up and down the back stairs, pretending to be Mrs. Goodhue and scaring Irene?"

"No—no, I wasn't," Joe protested. "That first night, I went down in those slippers to try and hear something. I knew Mother had some scheme as soon as I saw you. I couldn't hear anything, though, and I went back. It was the next night, after Mrs. Goodhue was found—I was hoping *Mother* would hear me. She was always so superstitious. I was sure I could frighten her home if she thought it was Mrs. Goodhue's spirit on the stairs."

"But you frightened my mother," Madeleine said wanly.

Joe drooped, and she went on, "I don't really understand. If Mrs. Goodhue was going to lay everything on the table, why did she put water in Bill's hair lotion?"

Joe's hands went up over his face and he moaned, "Oh, God!"

Bill snapped, "Joe!" and he dropped the hands and looked up. "What about the hair lotion?"

"Mother made that stuff up herself," Joe said despairingly. "She used to sell it around. I know she sold some to Mrs. Goodhue for you. She must have put the water into the bottle she sold Mrs. Goodhue, so that your hair would stick up and look like her photograph."

"So Mrs. Goodhue bought your cosmetics?" Eliot said languidly. "What else? Ties? Socks? Did she measure your arms and legs and buy your suits, too?"

"Supposing she had? I'm turned out as well as you."

"No, you're not," Madeleine said. "Eliot takes extra care with his appearance, and it shows. You should go with him when you buy your clothes."

"I wouldn't go with him if it meant walking around in a Buster Brown suit," Bill said disgustedly. "I'll go with you, though, after we're married."

"'Struth!" Eliot muttered. "You *are* going to marry her? Madeleine, my dear, how on earth did you get him to throw caution to the winds this way? Take on such a tremendous responsibility as marriage?"

"Oh, well—" She gave him a watery half smile. "Once a bully, always a bully, I suppose."

THE END

About the Rue Morgue Press

"Rue Morgue Press is the old-mystery lover's best friend, reprinting high quality books from the 1930s and '40s."
—*Ellery Queen's Mystery Magazine*

Since 1997, the Rue Morgue Press has reprinted scores of traditional mysteries, the kind of books that were the hallmark of the Golden Age of detective fiction. Authors reprinted or to be reprinted by the Rue Morgue include Catherine Aird, Dorothy Bowers, Pamela Branch, Joanna Cannan, Glyn Carr, Torrey Chanslor, Clyde B. Clason, Joan Coggin, Manning Coles, Lucy Cores, Frances Crane, Norbert Davis, Elizabeth Dean, Michael Gilbert, Constance & Gwenyth Little, Morris West, Marlys Millhiser, James Norman, Stuart Palmer, Craig Rice, Kelley Roos, Charlotte Murray Russell, Maureen Sarsfield, Margaret Scherf and Juanita Sheridan.

To suggest titles or to receive a catalog of Rue Morgue Press books write P.O. Box 4119, Boulder, CO 80306, telephone 800-699-6214, or check out our website, www.ruemorguepress.com, which lists complete descriptions of all of our titles, along with lengthy biographies of our writer